FIRST FIX YOUR ALIBI

*A Selection of recent titles from Severn House
by Bill James*

BETWEEN LIVES
DOUBLE JEOPARDY
MAKING STUFF UP
LETTERS FROM CARTHAGE
OFF-STREET PARKING
FULL OF MONEY
WORLD WAR TWO WILL NOT TAKE PLACE
NOOSE
SNATCHED

The Harpur and Iles Series

VACUUM
UNDERCOVER
PLAY DEAD
DISCLOSURES
BLAZE AWAY
FIRST FIX YOUR ALIBI

FIRST FIX YOUR ALIBI

Bill James

CRÈME de la CRIME

This first world edition published 2016
in Great Britain and the USA by
Crème de la Crime, an imprint of
SEVERN HOUSE PUBLISHERS LTD of
19 Cedar Road, Sutton, Surrey, England, SM2 5DA.
Trade paperback edition first published 2016
in Great Britain and the USA by
SEVERN HOUSE PUBLISHERS LTD.

British Library Cataloguing in Publication Data

James, Bill, 1929- author.
  First fix your alibi. – (The Harpur and Iles series)
  1. Harpur, Colin (Fictitious character)–Fiction. 2. Iles,
  Desmond (Fictitious character)–Fiction. 3. Drug dealers–
  Fiction. 4. Revenge–Fiction. 5. Police–Great Britain--
  Fiction. 6. Detective and mystery stories.
  I. Title II. Series
  823.9'14-dc23

ISBN-13: 978-1-78029-082-9 (cased)
ISBN-13: 978-1-78029-566-4 (trade paper)
ISBN-13: 978-1-78010-742-4 (e-book)

All Severn House titles are printed on acid-free paper.

Severn House Publishers support the Forest Stewardship Council™ [FSC™],
the leading international forest certification organisation.
All our titles that are printed on FSC certified paper carry the FSC logo.

MIX
Paper from
responsible sources
FSC FSC® C013056
www.fsc.org

Typeset by Palimpsest Book Production Ltd.,
Falkirk, Stirlingshire, Scotland.
Printed and bound in Great Britain by
TJ International, Padstow, Cornwall.

ONE

R alph Wyvern Ember, sole owner of the Monty social club in Shield Terrace, and chairman and chief executive of one of the most gilt-edged recreational substance firms in Britain, had watched, several times over the years, TV movie channel showings of a 1950s Alfred Hitchcock film called *Strangers On A Train* starring Farley Granger and Robert Walker. Although Ember had always enjoyed the film, even on his third and fourth viewing, he'd never found the plot entirely believable. It was a story – a good story – and stories could sometimes be a bit far-fetched, especially good stories. To give the audience a surprise, a thrill, they had to stretch situations and characters, sometimes too much.

But now, suddenly, he'd been forced to think the tale wasn't so basically incredible after all. This shook him. One of the main points about Ralph was that, although he considered himself reasonably mild and balanced, it always got right up his fucking nose if someone he knew well asked him to snuff out someone he hardly knew at all, or possibly someone he hadn't even heard of until this rather off-colour request. Such an approach irritated Ralph for two strong reasons. First, he had never been a hitman, even in his earliest, freewheeling commercial days. Unfortunate fatal spats with enemies had taken place but only very rarely; definitely nothing to write home about, encrypted. Second, suppose he *had* been an apprentice hitman at this youthful, tyro stage, as part of the business initiation process, his earned eminence in local society now, as compared to then, made that type of violence by Ralph more or less unthinkable currently. Or possibly more than more or less. Good God, the local evening paper often published very constructive, vigorously sincere letters from him on environmental and pollution topics over the signature Ralph W. Ember. Industrial effluent secretly discharged into rivers was something else that got up his nose. And then, consider the proprietorship of the Monty, his club bought from fine trading profits, for which he had many substantial ambitions.

Could he be expected immediately to shelve every other concern and narrow his intentions right down to a slaying? 'Untoward' was the word that came to Ralph's mind: surely, this kind of demand could be seen as nothing but untoward. Indelicacy Ralph detested. How could a friend, or friends, and/or a colleague, or colleagues – probably very familiar, long-term, with Ralph's true updated character – how *could* they imagine he'd jump to take on a blast job to head or chest-area despite his distinguished OBE'ish reputation now?

The *Strangers On A Train* film, and possibly the book it came from, started with – well, started with strangers on a train, Granger and Walker. The fact that they *were* strangers is the key element. Walker proposes to Granger that they each do a killing on behalf of the other. Ralph considered it not the usual kind of amiable chat that springs up between train passengers. Granger wants to get rid of his wife, and Walker will carry out the job on her. As *his* side of the deal, Granger will see off Walker's nuisance father for him. Because the victims and the murderers would be completely unknown to each other there'd be no obvious motives to guide the police. And at the time of the killings the husband and son will make sure to have well-attested, utterly uncrackable alibis. Walker more or less hypnotizes Granger with the lovely neatness of the ploy. They could each glory in a perfect crime.

Ralph Ember used to wonder whether anyone could really dream up such a devilish plan. And yet here, now, an extremely notable local business figure, Manse Shale, had approached Ember with what sounded like something from the very same production line. Yes, Ralph was shaken, and then disgusted. Ember's objections had to do with his rating as a man, and with his personal dignity. For ever, Ralph strove to further his rating as a man and to safeguard his personal dignity. Vital. A compulsion. Nobody else could look after your rating as a man and personal dignity for you. Keep non-stop watchful. Set yourself brilliant standards to achieve and achieve them.

So, he resented being thought casually available, like some sort of shoulder-holster, short-time tart. He'd always tried rigorously to prevent tarts working from the Monty, and this made the treatment of himself as a biddable body particularly offensive. Ralph recognized that these girls had to make a living, and that they wouldn't be doing it unless they had to; but he wouldn't allow the Monty to become a pick-up joint. That kind of publicity could really set him back.

When it came to a philosophy of life, Ralph saw himself as what was called 'an existentialist'. At first, he'd found this word tricky and difficult to remember. He did not go about blurting it to customers in the club. But the important thing to keep in mind was that, from the spelling, it obviously concerned existence, namely, in this case, Ralph's. He understood the term to mean you took total, unfaltering responsibility for your own behaviour, and you did not waver or call for aid from a vicar or a shrink or a rich aunty by marriage. Being recruited to do a killing for someone else definitely didn't at all fit in to that stern, flinty self-programming.

He had come across the term 'existentialist' during the foundation year of a mature student degree course begun at the local university. Points from the lectures on this subject lingered in his head, although he'd been forced by sharp business pressures to suspend the college course for now. Certainly, he regretted this break, but the continuing sweet surge in charlie and H used by so many professional folk with good, disposable incomes, recession or not, made his full-time, authoritative attention to the supply and distribution networks vital. This type of user-client tended to be intelligent and positive, and most had taught themselves efficient mainlining, and/or had bonny, powerful nostrils, still capable of clean-sweep, nicely directed, unwasteful snorts.

These cumulative factors could not be ignored and so Ralph had back-burnered the college programme. He saw the sacrifice as a *noblesse oblige* matter. Leadership of the company could not be safely delegated in these circumstances, and Ralph felt compelled to give his firm what the jargon would describe as 'hands on commitment', even though he had a very talented and dedicated crew of pushers, debt adjusters/enforcers, marksmen/women, couriers, etcetera; a normal personnel panoply for Ralph's type of enterprise. He regarded good personnel selection as one of his most fruitful flairs, and he did not need any of the big professional agencies to help him.

Existentialism insisted that every man and woman should try to control his/her own destiny through the application of his/her will. Ralph fervently agreed. And, in a strange, ironic way, he saw his decision temporarily to dump education and get back to dealing the top-grade merchandise as exactly this kind of self-commanding, existentialist decision; yes, even if it removed him from the teaching where he first learned to admire existentialism, and might have been able to learn more if he'd continued at the classes.

Although existentialism might tell him to apply his will and skills to the business, he did not think it would require him to kill an absolute stranger to Ralph whom Manse Shale happened to want slaughtered.

Naturally, the suggestion from Manse avoided blunt, straight-out language – not 'Ralph, how about terminating Frank Waverton for me, the ungovernable, scheming, dangerous, silky bastard?' Much more roundabout and gradual. To many the conversation might have sounded fairly run-of-the-mill and harmless. Ember spotted the real message, though. He prized his ability to see behind what people appeared to say, but which actually served only as surface, as decoy. This knack for delving to the essence he would sometimes think of as like that famous special typewriter designed to crack wartime German codes at Bletchley Park and featured in the film, *Enigma.*

Manse Shale and Ember had talked privately about what Ralph thought of as the *Strangers On A Train* idea after one of their fine, festive staff dinners. These occurred a couple of times a year. They took it in turns to pay the bill. The functions celebrated a unique trading alliance. Ralph and Manse ran similar healthy businesses selling recreational substances. Each operated within a clearly mapped area of the city and had an understanding that neither would infringe on the other's dedi-cated territory. Crude, self damaging and Adolfish – that's how they regarded the so-called 'turf wars' which could sometimes break out elsewhere, because one firm wanted another's ground and paying customers. Ralph and Manse aimed for profitable tranquillity and did all they could to prevent blood on the pavement. Ralph rejected as defeatist the idea that successful business practice necessarily excluded *civilized* business practice owing to inborn greed, jealousy and fear – fear of extinction if they didn't strike first.

One of the main police in the city, Assistant Chief Constable (Operations), Desmond Iles, let them know that as long as they maintained peace and put none of the public at crossfire risk he would allow them to carry on their trade. In Ralph's view, Iles could be a right, unpardonable, rude, brazen, malevolent prick, but he did have some reasonable ideas. He supported drugs legalization and practised his own unilateral version of that here, in wise cooperation with Ember and Shale. Iles never actually put this arrangement into words. The bugger was too smart for that. But he didn't act against them, and they could make a decently founded guess at his thinking. As Ralph's mother used to say, 'a nod's as good as a wink to a blind horse'. His mother had a whole barrelful of what some called clichés and others called folk wisdom. Ralph could take them or leave them alone.

Anyway, every sixth months or so the two companies held a sort of bonding, hearty dinner at the Agincourt Hotel, and it was following one of these happy feasts that Shale drew Ralph to a corner of the banqueting hall where they could talk. In Ember's opinion, that name Agincourt, marking a great British military victory way back in France, gave the evening occasion now a certain elegance and solid status. Didn't Laurence Olivier, mounted on an unblind white horse in the film *Henry V*, do the famous speech about the splendour of this imminent Agincourt battle?

The banqueting room had old-fashioned weapons fixed to the walls – halberds, pikes, longbows, lances, that kind of collection – to give a very pre-Hiroshima war atmosphere. They were only imitations, of course, and Ralph considered the display crappy; but the intention seemed good: a reminder of this country's great history and previous wholesome power. Although there was a free bar and unlimited, vintage wines on the tables, with liqueurs to follow, including Tia Marias, there had never been any trashing, any *major* trashing, of the hotel by Ralph's or Manse's people. Almost everyone recognized the calibre of the setting and respected it. Although Ralph knew that some crude jokers gave a changed version of the Olivier speech, altering 'Once more unto the breach, dear friends,' to what they termed the paedo theme song, 'Once more unto the crèche, dear friends,' that could be dismissed as grossly mischievous coarseness. There had been no instance of guests tearing the weaponry off the walls and staging their own plastic Agincourt battle, regardless of damage to the furniture and tableware. Nor, as far as Ralph knew, had there ever been any tit and/or bum groping of the waitresses, even though some wore cleavage dresses.

'I regard all this tonight as very much a milestone, Ralph,' Shale said. 'Milestones being a matter of undoubted progress; distance covered. This distance covered gives a promise, don't it, Ralph? The distance covered tells us that the distance to *be* covered in the future, *will* be covered because what has already been covered shows how the next bit of distance can be and will be covered.'

'Right,' Ember said. Manse had never been spot-on with grammar but he was not one to let that mess up expression of his very individual thoughts and ideas. He was short, square built with a snub face and a heap of dark hair. He had on today what Ralph recognized as a grey, double-breasted Paul Mixtor-Hythe three-piece suit that would have cost at least £1500. He alternated between this kind of outfit and others he'd picked up at Oxfam or the People's Dispensary For Sick Animals. He'd heard that families of dead noblemen, when clearing the wardrobes, sent these old, thick, long-lasting, beautifully cut, beigish suits to charity shops. Ferret-like was how Ember thought of Shale's eyes.

'I see mutuality here, Ralph,' he said.

'That's interesting.'

'Interdependence. Triumphs, difficulties in common.'

'Certainly,' Ralph said.

'When I speak of progress, what do you think I mean, Ralph?'

'Well, I suppose—'

'I mean expansion, consolidation, commercial invincibility.'

'These are fine objectives, Manse.'

This was one of the things about Shale: he could come out with big words at times, syllables piling up, and usually meaning what he thought they meant. It was some of the smaller words that floored him.

'And if that progress is endangered, put at bad risk, this is where the mutuality comes in, the interdependence, don't it?' Manse said.

'I think I—'

'We deal jointly, effectively, mercilessly with whatever, whoever, might be bringing that danger and risk. This mutuality is no simple matter, Ralph. This interdependence could also require what we might call interweaving. I look around this fine room, Ralph, and see the halberds, the pikes, the swords and scimitars as décor and think to myself that conflict in them days was a straightforward thing. If you got a longbow arrow in your eye this would deter any further warrior-like participation for at least the time being. Conflict in our day, Ralph, can be not simple at all. It might, in fact, require the interweaving I believe I mentioned earlier.'

'Yes, you did.'

'No dismal narrowness.'

'Dismal narrowness would be a mistake. But in what sense dismal narrowness, Manse?'

'One person's difficulty, problem, might require a solution, a remedy, from someone else. This, Ralph, is that mutuality. This is opportunism, but opportunism of a sound nature.'

'I'm not too clear what's being said here, Manse,' Ember replied. And this was true, except that Ralph felt sure something perilous and possibly sick would emerge eventually from the blabber.

'Opportunity. Catch-as-catch can,' Shale replied.

'Catch what as catch can, though?'

'This opportunity might present itself in totally random style. In fact, that's the beauty of it.'

'What is, Manse?'

'The randomness. Or the *apparent* randomness.'

'The randomness is not really random?' Ralph asked. 'This randomness is mock randomness, like gaming machines?'

'Me, I don't like the term "mock". It seems to say "false". I would rather say *created* randomness, scheduled randomness, but only those aware of the schedule would know this seemingly

random activity was, in fact, planned and devised, the outcome
worked for, selected, and very specific. It's like God and the
universe. Events happen that look to us, all of us, including *Old
Moore*'s *Almanac*, like accidental, random, out of nowhere. And
yet there might be a system to it all.'

'"God moves in a mysterious way; his wonders to perform?"'
Ralph said.

'You made that up, just this minute? Yes, like that, yes.'

'You've got some difficulty you want me to handle for you,
I gather, Manse,' Ember said, kindness in his tone, not shell
shock from the wordage.

'I've had tragedy in my life, Ralph,' Shale replied.

'Certainly.' Manse's second wife and young son were shot
dead in a mistaken attack during the school run.[1] The target
should have been Manse himself, but there had been a change
of routine and the gunman didn't adjust. Shale's daughter,
Matilda, survived.

'Yes, of course, you'll remember it, Ralph. There is a wonderful,
caring side to you, despite the occasional very justified, though
regrettable, need to do a wipeout.'

'Decorum is something I hold dear,' Ember said. He gave this
a matter-of-fact quality, no booming bombast, which he felt
would have been daft in someone keen on decorum.

'You are a famed supporter of the slogan "live and let live",
unless, naturally, some slimy, indecorous sod should not be let
live, which can be the case in our day-to-day experience. This
is the point I'm trying to get at, Ralph.' Ember, who was paying
tonight, had ordered a bottle of Kressmann's Armagnac to be
put on the table with balloon glasses and they both took mouth-
fuls now. Shale probably wouldn't know the difference in
quality between this and sarsaparilla, but he did a small nod
or two to signal recognition of something élite. Then he said,
'Following that disaster I withdrew to religion, seeking solace
and reassurance.'

'Yes, I know, Manse.'

'Donations.'

'This I can well believe.'

---

[1] See *I Am Gold*

'To the church.'

'Yes.'

'The roof fund. And extensive new flagstoning near the main doors. I felt fucking privileged to be a part of it, not full-out saintly, but positive.'

'I know the vicar and so on were very grateful.'

'I couldn't of gone on with the trading, not at that stage, Ralph. It would of seemed what-you-call?'

'Inappropriate.'

'That, yes. Or worse.'

'Disrespectful?'

'The pews,' Shale replied.

'Well, yes, most churches have many a pew.' This could happen to Ember if he talked with Manse for a long while: Ralph would amble almost as far into gobbledegook as Shale did.

'The pews are solid wood,' Manse replied, 'not your three-ply sheets sandwiching bubble wrap. Mahogany, mostly, or sapele.'

'Pews have to be able to take the weight,' Ralph said.

'Utterly true. At a wedding or funeral of someone popular, that could be a lot of arses on one pew. The pew got to be able to cope with this load, and some members of the congregation might be rotund or great with child and so offering extra pressure. It wouldn't be a laughing matter if one of them pews collapsed during a solemn service, people on the floor higgledy-piggledy, the best man disturbed by the noise so he drops the ring, him and the vicar scrambling about on the floor looking for it. Well, yes, it *would* be a laughing matter but it shouldn't be.

'If you're solo, though, in one of them pews, it being no special day in the church, you can feel sort of safe with that intensely genuine wood all around you, like a mahogany den, and that curved bit on the end as if cutting you off from the aisle and the rest of the church. Meditation a possible. Sometimes when I was boxed in and secure, with a nice little cushion for your knees, if wanted, I'd have precious, uninterrupted holy-silent minutes to wonder what mangy fucker put the word somewhere about which streets was used for the school run. All right, that tip was wrong re the driver and passengers because

I wasn't on the trip, but the geography was right, dead right. Dead.

'In my private little timber cell nun-like I would think that if one more detail had been correct in the information I would not be in my little timber cell that day enjoying the consolation of a blessed church. I would already of been in a different kind of timber cell. Rest In Pieces.'

'You believe you were betrayed?'

'As many most probably know, including you, Ralph, religion have got an item called a revelation.'

'The last book in the bible – *Revelation*.'

'Being part of religion at that period of my life, Ralph, I had a revelation. A name come into my head. Obviously, this is why I spoke of the mahogany.'

'Quite.'

'That kind of closed-off, solid capsule in the pew was a first-class site for one deeply personal revelation to yours truly. Privileged. Divine-sourced? Who can tell? But, anyway, it arrived.'

'Which name, Manse?'

'Besmirched, Ralph,' Shale replied.

'A strong word, Manse. In which particular? You feel, felt, besmirched? How was that?'

'Not so much self, Ralph.'

'I'm glad. You deserve no such suffering.'

'That name, suddenly brought to me in a sanctified setting – I felt it besmirched the very structure, fabric, atmosphere of a blameless church.'

'You were obviously in a profound religious state at that time. I think of Cardinal Newman and "lead kindly light", when an epiphany came to him to do with leaving the Protestant church.'

'There are some first-rate epiphanies about, Ralph. Yes, profound is right. I believe if I had not been in that profound state I might not of received the name and how to deal with it.'

'Ah, I didn't realize you'd been advised how to deal with it.'

'That's the beauty of religion, Ralph. If you ever come across it you'll discover that it recognizes there is rubbish in the world but it also tells you how to get rid of it. I saw during this specially delivered revelation in the church, like coming from my sub-conscious, that there's an old film called *Stranglers On A Train*.'

'I think it's "Strangers".'

'Whatever. To do with death, anyway. To do with death and with that recently referred to mutuality and interweaving.'

'It's a crazy plot, couldn't possibly be to do with real life.'

'When I gets a vision in a church, Ralph, I think of it as being full of accuracy.'

'But it had the name of the film wrong.'

'Neither here nor there. Merely I made an error in the label. We know what its message is, don't we? Its message is mutuality, interweaving and interdependence. The name is Frank Waverton, Ralph.'

Ember spelled it out audibly but not loudly: 'W-A-V-E-R-T-O-N? No, not a name I know. Should I? Never met him, I'm sure.'

'Dark hair worn short. Six foot two, 190 pounds. Mid-thirties. White. Long face. Off-and-on moustache, better off. Fitness freak. Does remote hill-path jogging early mornings like a boxer, all weathers. Swank dresser. Nothing off-the-peg. Specially crafted Charles Laity shoes.'

'No. Haven't come across him. He's here tonight?'

'Of course. But it's best like that.'

'Best like what, Manse?'

'Best you didn't know him.'

'Why?' Ember could see the answer to this, if Shale were thinking of the *Stranglers On A Train*. But Ralph longed for some clarity after all the verbiage and mahogany.

Shale said, 'Obviously, you've got to get to know him, but only in that one certain sense.'

'Which?'

'To recognize him. How could you help with the removal if you didn't know who was to be removed?' Shale had a good old chuckle at that total craziness. He drank a drop more Kressmann's, maybe to numb himself a little and forestall hysterics. In a while he said, 'But to identify someone is not the same as knowing them, is it, Ralph? Identity's an outside thing but *knowing* is something else. Knowing got depth.

Knowing is a connection, maybe a long-term connection. And that's the kind of connection murder-squad detectives would be looking for if Waverton got discovered somewhere of your choice, Ralph, and at a time of your choice, dead, by the method of your choice, a totally free hand re that.

'Police would be inclined to suppose there must be a reason for this abrupt, very assisted death, and the reason could be that one of them connections turned sour and kill-prone. Of course, Ralph, they'd be right: one of his connections, such as self, *would* of turned sour and kill-prone. But this connection, that is, self, would be nowhere near the execution venue having arranged, very neat, to be somewhere else at the moment of life extinction, as certified by qualified doctors; this somewhere else having excellent, absolutely clean-sheet witnesses, plural. Alibi fodder.'

'I fear this is hardly my type of work these days, Manse.'

'Hardly is right. This is a hard situation and it got to be dealt with in a hard fashion. But there's a nicer side to it, also. It's not all about self, me, is it?'

'Isn't it?'

'There'll come a time when you're in this type of bother-someness – a destruction of someone needed, in a good cause. At that moment who gladly, commitedly, steps forward? Self once more, but self now acting for *your* self in reciprocity. We got a touch of the *quid pro quoism* here, Ralph, which is Latin for "You scratch my back, I'll scratch yours," as often spoken in a hot old Latin city like Rome owing to insect bites.'

TWO

But, of course, Ralph didn't – couldn't – completely fool himself, or, in fact, fool himself very much at all. He knew that he hadn't left the rougher side of his life completely behind. Impossible. He fully realized that his stacked money, and his sweet social position, and his club, and his children's non-state schooling and gymkhana ponies, and Low Pastures, his beautiful, historic manor house – OK, he knew the whole splendid lot depended on the commodities business: the illegal commodities in an illegal business, although locally tolerated so far by that accomplished tyrant, Iles.

Ralph was aware that he tried to dodge around the blunt, exact, unwholesome term 'drugs business', and went instead for the vague, would-be-harmless phrases, 'commodities business', or, sometimes, 'recreational substances business'. He didn't want too much definition of the game. He found the word 'drugs' ugly, almost a rhyme with ugly, in fact: that rough 'u' sound, and the spiky 'g'. Ugly and tainted. Some delicacy was surely needed. He liked to think that delicacy featured strongly in his DNA.

The fact that he had shelved the university course so he could give his full flair to the constantly expanding substances trade – there it was, one of those nice, cover-up words! – yes, his temporary withdrawal from classes showed he understood his priorities absolutely clearly. Further education was certainly important and he hoped to return to it. But, for now, it would be a bad distraction. He'd feel irresponsible. Margaret, Ember's wife, had always regarded Ralph's mature-age longing for a degree as pathetic, laughable tuft-hunting, anyway.

During that foundation year at the uni, Ralph had read a Shakespeare play where some lines really hit smack-on his present situation. They mentioned 'a tide in the affairs of men' which, if you caught it at high water, could carry you on to a fortune, like a bonny ship making real headway with its knots per hour. But if you missed this chance your life would be shallow and miserable. Ralph thought of the grass, coke and H sales at the moment as like that maximum, rolling tide. It would be mad to neglect the great prospects offered. Ember saw irony here: to maximize profits from the swelling flood of demands for the firm's stuff, he would be shelving college study of the very playwright who inspired him to do it, via 'the tide in the affairs of men' observation.

And, although he'd been offended, disgusted, at first by Manse Shale's death-shuffle proposal, he recognized that behind all his shambolic, roundabout jabber there was, as ever, a bright commercial brain and sharp instincts; maybe sharper because of the hurt he had suffered. If Manse saw serial treachery and malice in Waverton there'd probably *be* serial treachery and malice in Waverton. Manse claimed he'd received this eye-opener by a kind of supernatural, for-addressee-only, epistle in church. That was just a bit of fancy packaging for Shale's idea, though. His suspicions of Waverton as someone who had betrayed him, and might again, would have come to Manse no matter what the location. He didn't need help from a pew, intensely wooden or not. The point about Manse was that, if he'd gone religious for a spell, this would be fairly genuine while it lasted – matins, litanies, responses, use of the kneel-cushion, the whole devotional apparatus – but afterwards he'd want to show some definite personal gain from the effort he'd put in trying to believe; and from what he'd lashed out for the roof and flagstoning, as well as in the general Sunday service collections. He'd settle for a revelation, one that seemed to get the spelling right: W-A-V-E-R-T-O-N.

Ralph realized that some, looking at the Waverton–Manse situation, would say, 'OK, if there is a problem it's Manse Shale's problem, *his* wife and kid shot, and you, Ralph, shouldn't trouble yourself with it; definitely not to the point of destroying Waverton as first part of an interchange deal: a mutuality, mortuary deal.' But Ralph couldn't take that isolationist view of things. It went against his expansive nature.

At their corner table in the Agincourt, he found himself staring over the edge of his Armagnac glass as he took a sip, and trying to fix on someone answering the description of

Waverton provided by Manse. The room was crowded with people from the two firms, many with spouses or partners. Some were still at their tables chatting. Others stood now in groups, relaxed, conversational, notably unraucous so far, drinks in hand. Ember's wife, Margaret, would only very rarely attend the firm's social occasions – found them boring – and wasn't here tonight. And, of course, Manse had no wife or girlfriend since the shooting.

Ralph shortlisted three men who might be Waverton. He couldn't get more particular than that for now. He wouldn't ask Shale to help him with the sorting out, or let Manse see Ralph was doing an eye-trawl for likelies. Either of those reactions could indicate to Manse that Ralph might be interested. They'd be what police interrogators called 'buy signs', when a suspect gave hints he'd confess to get a softer sentence.

At present, Ralph must avoid any semblance of commitment. He had to stand by that pompous bit of phrasing he'd offered Shale just now: 'I fear this is hardly my type of work these days, Manse.' Pompous, no question, yet also, no question, true. Ralph couldn't allow himself to be tricked or dragged back into the area of outright trade violence, could he? Didn't some writer say the past was a different country? Ralph would like to keep it like that, at a far-off distance, but wasn't certain he could.

A couple of the men he'd selected were only back views and he had to make his guesses based on hair colour, fine tailoring, build and probable age. They were too far off for a shoes assessment. The other possible was front on, long-faced, perhaps booze reddened for now, well-garbed, but more like forty than thirties. Perhaps regular hooch had put some extra years on his skin. At any rate, to Ralph, it did not seem the sort of very ordinary, lumpen face that deserved to be ripped apart by pistol bullets. This squeamishness wasn't new for Ralph. Always, even including that novice, learning-curve stage in his business vocation, he had regarded it as distasteful to turn a gun on someone, although, as Manse had mentioned, there were occasionally very sound reasons to eliminate this or that, these or those, person, persons. Fine, but, until a few minutes ago, Ralph had been sure he'd moved into a sort of dignified, self-regulated life where the pressures from such 'very sound reasons' could no longer get at him. They used to come from that different country. But then, Manse arrives with a resurrection of this eerie, murderous, trade-off message from *Stranglers On A Train* via a nave or apse.

Not everyone would understand why Ralph couldn't regard Shale's possible troubles as Shale's, and only Shale's: *'I'm* all right, Jack,' or, in this case, *'I'm* all right, Manse.' Ember often recalled a spiel by that snotty, clever braggart, Assistant Chief Constable (Operations), Desmond Iles. During one of his routine bullying, disruptive calls at Ember's club, the Monty, accompanied as ever by his sidekick, Detective Chief Superintendent Colin Harpur, Iles had talked contentedly to a little group at the bar about the whole, wide, local business scene, and especially about Ralph's and Manse's firms. Strategy: Iles had the rank for that. He'd referred to 'equipoise' – just the kind of vain, big-word, mouthing Ralph would expect from this grandiose heap. But, because it was so poncey, the term had stuck in Ralph's mind, plus, virtually verbatim, a couple of sentences where it figured. Iles had been describing what he praised as the 'happy harmony' that existed because the two firms operated peacefully alongside each other in armed neutrality. 'But what if one of them gets damaged or even put entirely out of action?' he'd asked. As was quite usual with him he replied to his own question, because the know-all prick didn't feel anyone else would be intelligent and perceptive enough to do it; or intelligent and perceptive enough to give what he'd decided was the right answer, the *only* right answer.

'Suddenly we lack equipoise,' he'd said, 'because equipoise demands at least two components.' Really, though? What a terrific insight! 'Remove one and in the resulting lurch the city no longer benefits from those powerful, smooth-running, allied firms.' Iles obviously didn't want that kind of chaos. Neither did Ralph: probable vicious, all-out territorial warfare. The ACC had gone on to spout something like, 'Where there was amity and cooperation there would be hugger-mugger – another strange term that had lodged in Ember's memory – where there was light there would be pitch; where there was impeccable order there would be shit.'

'Mr Iles prefers the impeccable order,' Harpur had said. 'It's a forgiveable little kink of his.'

Ember, also, would prefer order to shit and, therefore, Manse's safety, health and durability were crucial. Senior people in Shale's firm had managed to keep it going reasonably well during Manse's lapse into religion and donations. That successful caretaking might not be possible next time, though, suppose there *were* a next time. Ralph must try to prevent this. If Waverton did amount to a continuing menace to Manse Shale's business, then Waverton had better be got rid of. A menace to Shale's company was a menace to Ralph's. The 'interweaving' ensured this. Did that mean Ralph would do the getting rid of so Shale couldn't be blamed for it? Did that also mean Ralph would do the getting rid of so as to build up credit for future use in a sort of reciprocal, 'you-owe-me-one, Manse', murders fund? Possibly.

This was how Ember's thinking had moved. But now, at the Agincourt celebration dinner: 'Oh, sorry, sorry, sorry, Ralph, Manse,' Assistant Chief Iles called out merrily as the folding table where Ralph and Shale had been talking skidded to the left and then collapsed. As if to demonstrate that powerful, glorious love of order mentioned recently by Harpur, Iles had flung across the big Agincourt banqueting hall a heavy who'd been posted to guard the door and keep out the uninvited. He'd dutifully attempted to stop Iles and Harpur. The man crashed into the corner table bringing it down, and staggered on a few paces, eventually striking his head against the bar and concussing himself.

'Well done, oh, so very well done, Ralph!' Iles shouted. Ember had managed to grasp the Kressmann Armagnac bottle in time so it didn't smash on the ground or spill. The balloon glasses did fall and break, though. 'Col and I thought we'd look in and make sure everything was hunky-dory. Harpur believes in maintaining amiable relations between us – the police – and the general population, which would include you and Manse.'

Iles turned the doorman on to his back, checked his tongue wasn't choking him, then straddled him and began to give mouth-to-mouth resuscitation. The ACC was in full, light blue, dress uniform, plus cap. The soles of his shoes showed very little wear.

Yes, Ralph saw some of that much desired, precious,

precarious orderliness in this scene. There was the flattened doorman wearing his dismal workaday denim lying stunned and useless alongside the toppled table and the glass splinters; and there was Iles in his natty power-blessed clothing and cap intent on restoring the pulverized bully-boy to life and normality. All right, Ralph had no fondness or respect at all for the wearer of that fine uniform, Iles, but the fine uniform was undoubtedly fine, with near-top-dog epaulettes, and seemed to proclaim dignity, rectitude, competence, benign control. Order, in fact. This uniform would look brilliant and reassuring at any official ceremony but did not seem out of place, either, therapeutically straddling a shattered, by-the-hour thug.

The man stirred and managed to get a small, pity-seeking moan out around Iles's lips. The ACC finished the mouth-to-mouth. Ralph would admit that Iles never persisted with a grievance against anyone. As long as he could throw someone who annoyed him the full width of a big room to crash against something nice and solid, with the possibility of a fractured skull, Iles would consider that quite enough to make his point.

'Come on, old chap, you've had a nasty little turn, that's all – probably the excitement of the Agincourt occasion,' he said, 'so many celebrities.' Iles swung his right leg over the body and stood up. He and Harpur bent to help the man get to his feet. They guided him a few steps and propped him against the bar. Iles called for something 'restorative and enhancing' and gave the man a tot of single malt. 'Good,' the ACC said.

Harpur righted the table and cleared the major pieces of glass away with his foot. He collected a couple more chairs and Iles, Ember, Shale and Harpur sat down again. Ember called to the barman to bring more glasses and the usual port and lemon for Iles – the 'old tart's drink', as he called it; and a double gin topped up with cider in a half pint glass for Harpur. Ralph and Manse drank some more of the Kressmann's.

The doorman went back to his post. 'Perhaps we should have let you know we were going to drop in, Ralph, Manse,' Harpur said. 'We don't usually. It's a long time since our last visit.'

'Col had begun to feel this was rather stand-offish, if not rude,' Iles said, 'so he insisted we come. Col is like that, a gem, very socially aware and keen not to give offence. One shares that feeling oneself, of course.' The doorman threw up noisily. 'Fucking Hollywood,' the ACC said. 'They can clear that up when they do the glass splinters. Yet he didn't taste too bad. You and Ralph were having a secluded little pow-wow, were you, Manse?'

'A kind of summing-up of the business and fiscal half-year,' Ember replied.

'Col felt it would be something like that,' Iles said.

'And the firms' pension funds,' Ralph said.

'Ah,' Iles replied. 'Col, counting the vehicles in the hotel car park just now, remarked to me, "This looks like a pensions discussion." Harpur has seen a great deal of life. He intuits. You'd be amazed at how frequently he intuits. Show him an array of expensive motors in a hotel car park and he'll say at once, "Pensions." If there were a Queen's Police Medal for intuits, he'd walk away with it.'

Of course, Ralph recognized this as micky-taking. It was in the style of this arrant, fully paid-up, degenerate sod, Iles. He would fix on a word or phrase launched by someone else and play about with it, pretending to take it seriously but really giving it big, Desilesian ridicule. Did he somehow have a true idea of what Ember and Manse had been discussing before the doorman came amongst them like grape shot?

Iles glanced about the room, smiling sort of genially. *His* sort of. He said to Ralph and Manse, 'I know Col thinks I should speak a few words. He won't tell me as much because it would impose obligation, and Col is not that kind of person – too considerate, too sensitive to others' feelings.'

'What do you mean, Mr Iles, "speak a few words"?' Ralph replied.

'Yes, a few words in celebration,' Iles said.

'"In celebration" of what?' Ralph asked.

'Yes, in celebration,' Iles answered. 'Col said to me the other day, "Do you realize, sir, that it's an age since we've been to one of the justly famed Agincourt meetings? This could be deemed dereliction. I feel we should get along there this time because the occasion is special. We should, in the words of the cricketing metaphor, break our recent duck, i.e., reach something more than nil visits this year".'

'But in which way is the occasion special?' Ralph asked.

'And this is how we come to be in the very well-occupied car park and led to deduce that serious discussion must be under way, such as at least pensions,' Iles replied enthusiastically.

'Why do you say "at least", Mr Iles?' Ralph asked. He feared that the otherwise cheerful evening could be spoiled – first the shattered, vomiting doorman; and then Iles with his 'few words'. Which fucking few words? Would they really be few? Would they be civilized, tolerable? Notoriously, he would take over public occasions, sometimes forcibly, particularly funerals, though other gatherings, too. When he spoke of 'a special occasion' it might mean he was going to get difficult and turbulent in one of his own 'special' ways. Ralph didn't fancy this.

Iles stood now and rapped the table with his knuckles. The room went silent. Everyone faced him. 'Dear friends,' he said, 'Col and I are here tonight to mark the return of Manse Shale to this city's mercantile scene after the disastrous ambush where his wife and son were killed and, following that, his period of spiritual restitution and repair. Isn't it wonderful to see him back in the esteemed role he occupies so brilliantly?' Iles slowly, solemnly raised his glass of port and lemon and said, 'Let us all drink to Manse Shale and to his triumph over hellishness.'

'To Manse!' the crowd called out and followed Iles in the toast. Shale stood, too, now and gave a slight bow first to Iles and then to the general assembly. The moment had dignity and quiet splendour. It made Ralph think of television coverage of a royal wedding in Westminster Abbey. A quantity of dark hair fell forward on to Shale's brow and he brushed it back gently, unhurriedly, with his right hand. This gesture did not seem to Ralph showy or vain. Manse might have learned something about humility from sermons in his recent church era. There were more cries of acclamation and some applause. Ember considered that, despite Shale's suffering, his eyes retained their undiluted ferretiness. Manse had a formidable inner strength.

Iles said, 'What else can I feel for Harpur but major gratitude? He persuaded me in his tactful yet determined fashion to attend your function tonight and enjoy the lovely sense of fellowship and conviviality, qualities that cannot be bettered, I'm sure, in any comparable get-together nationwide, if not even globally. Trade rivalries are put aside for the jolly duration of fine feasting and are temporarily replaced by happy, authentic comradeship.'

There were loud shouts of: 'Hear, hear!'

'And you know, folks,' Iles said warmly, 'as I look out on all these fond, cordial faces I think to myself that among them somewhere is the infinitely devious, contemptible arsehole who supplied the school run route for Naomi and Laurent's fated day of death. This was someone close, someone familiar, who got the occupants of the car wrong, but the street directions so cruelly right. If it wouldn't look like an unkind send-up of the nominal door bouncer, I could puke when I recall that plot against Manse. The gunman was killed at the time, so we got no leads from there. We know the firm he was hired from, but not who hired him. I, Desmond Iles, have to find the filthy, slimy whisperer. And from there I might discover who was ultimately in charge and got the whisper. Harpur will try to help me after his own lumbering, well-meant style. He has some good moments and not just diagnosing pensions discussions from a crowded car park.'

'Thank you, sir,' Harpur replied.

'That's not really a skill there's much call for following the great Parliamentary Reform Act of 1832,' Iles said. 'It wouldn't appear on Col's CV: *Qualified to infer pensions colloquia from hotel car parks.'*

He moved away from alongside Harpur. As was usual, Ralph had hired a disc jockey for dancing after the meal. He was about to start the music. But Iles stepped on to the little raised platform at the end of the banqueting hall, stood commandingly in front of the sound equipment, and announced that, if people didn't mind, he would like to show gratitude for being welcomed into the function by singing an aria from one of his favourite operas, *Madame Butterfly*. He admitted it was a song normally performed by a woman, but said he didn't care for sex restrictions. 'Music has no gender,' he stated. The number, he told the room, was 'One Beautiful Day' ('Un Bel Di') in which Butterfly dreams hopelessly – as we sense – for the return of Lieutenant Pinkerton, her rotten, double-crossing husband. Iles said that one male officer in uniform (himself) yearning for another male officer in uniform (Pinkerton) brought extra width and modernity to the opera. Rename it *ACDC Butterfly,* Ember thought.

He considered Iles got his mild tenor voice around the soprano notes and Italian wordage OK for the first few minutes but then gradually, unstoppably, broke down into desperate sobbing at the terrible sadness of Butterfly's fate. Ember thought it might not be the first time Harpur had witnessed this kind of pain engulf Iles. There must be weaknesses in the assistant chief's customary brass-necked, rough-house personality. Hurrying forward, Harpur seemed prepared for the collapse and brought an obviously very clean, very ready, white handkerchief from his pocket and methodically wiped tears from Iles's face, the ACC unresisting. Then Harpur helped him, still weeping, to a chair near the doorman's neatly strata-formed pile of sick. Possibly Harpur always stocked a clean-up, ministering hanky when he and Iles went to this type of function.

Harpur nodded to the disc jockey. He announced a Clean Bandit number that Ralph used sometimes at the Monty. People put their drinks glasses on the table and got out on to the patch of open floor.

'I could kill that bastard,' Iles said.

'Which?' Ralph asked.

'I think the ACC means the composer,' Harpur said, 'but he's probably already dead.'

'Why, why couldn't Puccini round it off right?' Iles said. 'This is a fifteen-year-old girl he's putting through the mincer.'

'They can be like that,' Ember said. 'Geniuses get through practising their scales and then look around for a tragedy to musicalize. It's to tweak our responses. They don't much care what the response is as long as they can achieve a tweak. It means they've reached us, like a town crier.' God, he hoped Harpur and Iles wouldn't turn up regularly at the Agincourt meets from now on. If they did, it would be wise to ask Iles for a different type of song, something hearty and assertive, such as 'Drake's Drum' or 'Tomorrow Is A Lovely Day'.

Shale gazed for more than a minute at a couple dancing nearby. Ralph gazed at them, too. The man was one of those whose backs he had taken note of a little while ago. Now, Ralph saw that his face and frontage matched pretty well Manse's description of Waverton. He did look fit enough for dawn jogs on remote hillsides. Ralph glanced away to Shale again. The ferrety eyes gave Ralph a non-blink stare and then swung left towards Harpur.

'How does the 1832 Parliament thing come into things?' Manse asked.

'Well, yes,' Harpur replied.

He and Iles left soon afterwards. Iles seemed to Ralph more or less all right again now, his sorrow and rage at the way Pinkerton had rejected him virtually under control.

THREE

In some ways, Ember didn't know what to make of that Agincourt evening, but in one crucial way he did: he knew Manse Shale's *Strangers On A Train* idea now definitely required thinking about; thinking seriously about. There had been, first, the confirmation by Iles that Manse correctly assumed betrayal from within Shale's own firm had probably led to the killing of his wife and son in the school-run Jaguar. If Iles believed something *you'd* better think about believing it, too. He might be an evil prat – no, certainly *was* an evil prat – but under the braided cap a busy brain functioned; a destructive, continuously malicious, egomaniac brain, but, still, a brain.

Of course, Shale went further and claimed to have identified the traitor, Frank Waverton. Iles did not endorse this in his 'few words' but had spoken as if the two-timer were in the Agincourt room. He hadn't indicated male or female. True, he'd called the renegade an arsehole but, like music, arseholes were not gender specific. They got allocated willy-nilly.

Obviously, Iles might know more than he said. Police usually did, and especially top police, and even more especially among top police, Iles. Just the same, Ralph doubted whether Iles had the name, and Ember couldn't himself feel totally sure Manse was right: that sudden visionary gift sent special-delivery through the church didn't strike Ralph as convincing; sort of: 'Vengeance is mine,' saith the Lord. 'I'm willing to share it this once with you, though, Manse.'

But Ember could accept now that someone, probably from within Shale's firm, had tried to sell Manse to an enemy, might try to sell him again, and had to be stopped, preferably and non-traceably by Ralph. This was the tricky, troublesome part of the thinking – the 'by Ralph' bit. That had also been confirmed at the Agincourt, not in the same straightforward fashion, however.

What had disturbed Ember was the kind of silliness and lack

of focus infecting the police people whose job it was to hunt down all accessories to the Jaguar ambush. Ralph had come to consider that he was the only one with the commitment and drive to clinch this. Commitment and drive Ralph suspected were as central to him as circulation of the blood. Shale, in that sequence of stares, first at Waveton, if that's who the dancer was, then at Ralph, seemed to acknowledge Ember's special zest and competence. Manse obviously considered that if Ralph did a murder for him it would be a beautiful, deft, nicely managed murder which, as it were, called out for reciprocity, though without stipulating date and time.

Iles had spoken of the need to fix blame, but surrounded that basic, vital matter with the absurd, stagey, blubbing grief from his transsexual performance as Madame Butterfly, and the nonsensical, irrelevant reference to Harpur's CV, and to parliament in history. Harpur was nearly as bad. Manse had asked him very reasonably how this mention tied in with everything else about the current parking and pensions, and Harpur answered, 'Yes' – except it offered no answer at all but a haughty brush-off. Ralph would admit 'yes' was a word built to be an answer, but not to the kind of question Manse had asked. Often he'd noticed examples of anti-communication between Harpur and Iles: there'd be questions, there'd be replies, but they rarely had much to do with each other, like ships that passed in the night.

Ralph retained the conviction that he, alone, or maybe with Manse to some degree – yes, Ralph retained the conviction that only the pair of them possessed a proper approach to the current, pressing realities. And Ralph felt proud of this. It made him think again, but more strongly than ever before that his present fine flamboyant life – the wealth, the property, the club, the ponies, the private schooling etcetera – all of it was frippery, wholly, secretly, dependent on this other world of conflict, threat, ruthless gain, violence. He felt thankful to the Agincourt for helping him see these factors in their true shape, and to work out how to deal with them. It would be inane not to recognize unpleasant, tricky truths and take them into the reckoning. That kind of evasiveness was certainly not how the battle of Agincourt had been resoundingly won.

Such thinking chimed with a lesson Ember had taught himself during his university time. He'd decided then that he hated the Romantic poets, as they were called, such as Keats and Shelley, for being stupidly fanciful and escapist. They said the world was so horrible to them, cruel and cramping, they'd like to be something else, such as a nightingale or a skylark, to soar out of it all. They barmilly longed for the impossible – to ditch their human frames and get feathers. And, talking of the barmy, apparently there was even a French Romantic poet whose lover demanded that Time should go more slowly, or maybe stop altogether, because she and the poet were having such a great intimacy session at a lake and didn't want it to end; maybe she took a long while to come. But, on the other hand, very kindly, she asked Time to move super-fast for all people in a bad way and suffering, so it would be over for them sooner. There'd be two kinds of clock, would there, one whizzing around like a greyhound after the rabbit, the other taking a couple of hours to do a minute, or not budging at all? Crazy! Down at the lake if someone asked what time it was the answer might be 'half past three yesterday' in French.

Ralph preferred other, earlier writers, such as Alexander Pope and Jonathan Swift. In fact, he cherished a bond with their sort, and thought they'd approvingly spot a similarity with themselves in him. They also saw the world was lousy, but they didn't want to fly away, cheeping their rhymed misery in verses, but tried to improve matters here below, tried to put things right, mainly by mocking in their work all the wrongdoing and prescribing change. Now, although Ralph couldn't do satire of this quality, he thought he might get the same type of brave facing up to things by duly slaughtering Waverton *for* Manse, with another death *by* Manse in the pending tray.

FOUR

When looking back on the Agincourt evening, Ralph had another point to take into account. As Ember was leaving, Shale had asked in a really cuddlesome tone, 'Why don't you look in at my home, Ralph, Wednesday evening, nine fifteen?'

This had enraged Ralph, especially the terse, non-negotiable exactness of the nine fifteen. Not 'about nine fifteen', or 'nine fifteen'ish', but stark, obligatory 'nine fifteen'. Was that the way to speak to the owner of a country estate and a social club, and who wrote constructive letters to the press on environmental topics as Ralph W. Ember? It had come across as an instruction, Ember thought – left him no room to mull whether this was convenient. Convenient? Although coated in slob smarm it sounded like, 'Fuck convenience, Ralph, fuck mulling, just make sure you get there on the dot.' Perhaps it could be seen as typical of Manse's whole attitude in the Waverton affair. Shale seemed to behave as if the entire kill project had been agreed in fundamentals and now it was time to get at the details.

Well, not 'now' in the Agincourt, but next Wednesday at nine fifteen prompt, if you please, and if you don't. Ralph felt he was being squeezed into Shale's crowded, distinguished appointments diary as a rare favour, and should bloody-well rejoice at his good luck: *nine p.m. Vladimir Putin, nine fifteen Ralphy.* Manse had shaped the invitation as a question – 'Why don't you look in?' etcetera. Ralph saw this as tactics, as trickery, to suggest Manse wasn't issuing an order, a command. He damn well was, though. Ralph could see through that crude ploy.

Despite fearing his precious and powerful free will was under attack by Shale, Ralph had agreed to make the visit. But he'd be watchful for any further attempts at disguised diktat. His mind had certainly been moving towards acceptance of Shale's plan for finishing off Waverton, yes, but he would resist any enforced haste, any frogmarching. He had an image to guard.

He could not be conned or bullied or taken for granted. Many
had discovered this. After so much time in tandem, why hadn't
Manse, for God's sake? It made Ralph question whether the
seemingly decent live-and-let-live understanding between Shale
and him had real worth. A show, little more? This meeting at
the rectory was presumably to talk over the run-up to the
Waverton project. All right, but Manse had better not try
imposing methods and means on him.

The 'nine fifteen, Wednesday' wasn't the only part of this
arrogant invitation that infuriated Ralph. 'Why don't you look
in at my *home*?' Shale had said. 'Home!' That was a trifle
weighty and puffed-up, wasn't it? Couldn't he have said something casual like 'my place' or 'my house'? After all, his 'home'
didn't amount to much when seen against Ralph's spread, Low
Pastures, surely. Of course, Ember had decided only a short
while ago that pride in his property, civic distinction and wealth
was ridiculous and based on self-deception. But this terse, bossy
bit of behaviour by Shale – 'Why don't you look in at my
home. Wednesday evening, nine fifteen p.m.' – pushed Ember
back towards that foolish pride in possessions and reputation.
This helped increase Ralph's anger. It made him feel unstable,
inconstant, weak. He found he couldn't stop himself making
comparisons, so as to bring Manse down from his pathetically
pompous position to where he should be.

Shale's *home* was once the St James's church rectory. Manse
had told Ember that he liked to sit in what he called 'the den
room' doing his business accounts for raves and street sales
and think that in former times the rector might have written
sermons and testimonials for parishioners there. Manse felt
that this gave his own work a certain sacredness. He said there
were times when he felt God was actually present doing a
Jehovah-type hover in the den room, having returned to look
for the rector, omniscience temporarily on the blink; but, once
that was remedied, God had seemed quite ready to accept Shale
instead, realizing change could occur anywhere. Almost
everyone Ralph knew in the substances trade wanted to break
through ultimately, or sooner, into respectability, and even
holiness. Manse thought he could start that advance by owning

a rectory, with its connection to St James's church and St James himself, whom Shale had discovered wrote at least one Epistle in the New Testament and – very important as an associate of Manse – was nicknamed 'The Just'. Ralph would choose a different route to stainless status via (a) obviously, he could not really discount his venerable manor house, Low Pastures; (b) the glorious Monty improvement schedule; (c) his vigilant, articulate, published concern for the environment.

Ralph reacted very positively to the crackle of the gravel under his tyres as he drew up at nine fifteen on Wednesday evening at the Old Rectory. Ralph felt certain that, as gravel went, this would be extremely high calibre, probably dredged from a very select underwater site near Flat Holm in the Bristol Channel and freighted here by lorry or rail for customers who wouldn't baulk at the special delivery price, such as Manse. He had to have the best. He was trying to catch up. Ralph wouldn't congratulate him on the plumpness and attractively variegated colours of the gravel because that would sound patronizing. Shale had to regard that gravel as if it were the only type of gravel he could possibly think of. Other gravels would be the equivalent of plonk in the wine scene, as against a grand vintage. This gravel told of Manse's social ranking. No, not of his *actual* social ranking, but the social ranking he wanted. Ralph could sympathize to a degree with this ambition. Ember, too, believed social ranking should be a continuing progress, and he would seek unwaveringly to improve the quality of his various interests to help with this worthwhile mission.

The rectory was certainly sizeable, but, to Ember's mind, deeply ordinary: a tall, gaunt job in grey stone. It couldn't be described as actually historic because almost certainly it only went back to the Victorian era, whereas Low Pastures had existed for many centuries: at different periods a lord lieutenant of the county had lived there and the Spanish consul, and most probably a squire or two. Oliver Leach (Caring Oliver) a tireless villain with a wealthy wife, had it just before Ralph, but only very briefly. 'Caring' had died a while ago.

Manse's new blue Jaguar stood near the house now. In the rather measly porch were two bicycles, one a modern mountain bike for serious outings; the other a 1930s style Humber with a Sturmey Archer three-gear stout rear hub and an encased chain. Manse liked to do a trundle around the centre of the city on this now and then. Perhaps it was a family heirloom and he had to keep it in a decent, working state.

Shale opened the front door himself. His daughter, Matilda, stood a little way behind him in her school blazer, blue, trimmed with black. Whatever social class objectives he might have, it seemed Manse didn't dress up for them at home. He wore a shagged-out, unshapely beige cardigan with bulbous, mock-leather buttons, old, wide-legged khaki slacks, and brown slippers.

Standing like this, slightly ahead of Matilda in the porch, and smiling an unconditional welcome, Shale looked fatherly, not at all like a murder impresario. Ralph felt half-sorry he had thought of him just now as a slob. Manse *was* in some aspects a slob but Ralph saw something noble and occasionally touching in the way he tried not to be. Manse had some self-awareness, and Ralph thought that to be self-aware of a self like his must be tough. And, of course, Manse grieved still and Ember tried to show continuous tenderness towards him, slob or not.

To view these two, Shale and his daughter, at the door of the biggish property, with the large rectory hall behind them, was bound to emphasize the awful fact that half the family had been annihilated, leaving a huge quantity of space. And, previous to that, the children's mother had abandoned them and Manse to join some indeterminate lover in, possibly, Rhyl.

Matilda said, 'I was pleased when Daddy told me you were coming tonight at nine fifteen, Mr Ember. It will be nice and very kind if you could call more often. I think Daddy gets lonely. Our mother is gone for keeps and then Naomi gets killed like that with Laurent in the earlier Jag. Naomi was not our mother and so we could refer to her as Naomi.'

'We'll go into my den room, shall we?' Manse said in a tone ablaze with geniality and respect. 'Such a visitor as Ralph fully deserves that, doesn't he, Matty?'

'I sincerely believe he does,' she replied. 'What I would like is that this visit should not be only about work but more to do with friendship, and so Mr Ember would come here more frequently for conversations on very numerous, worldwide topics. And perhaps Daddy could come to *your* house, for other conversations, Mr Ember, to take his mind off closer things.'

'I'll go and get some wine and orange squash from the fridge,' Shale replied. 'In this property there is no sexism. The domestic duties do not inevitably and always fall on the female, oh no. You two have a pleasant chat while I'm in the kitchen.'

Ralph wondered whether Manse meant a pleasant chat about snuffing out one of her dad's colleagues. Matilda and Ralph sat opposite each other in easy chairs. Matilda said, 'There used to be several friends of Daddy who would call and stay here for a while, weeks, sometimes even months – Carmel, Patricia, Lowri Billsborough – though only one at a time, naturally. And then they stopped, of course, when Naomi came. Now, they seem to have gone – married, perhaps, or that kind of thing. It's only natural. They couldn't wait around for ever, could they, and nobody would have known Naomi was going to get it like that by mistake, leaving such a gap? Carmel Arlington had a regular boyfriend, anyway. She knew a tremendous amount about porcelain and *Mein Kampf*.

'I and my brother, Laurent, now dead, knew Daddy's work might be dangerous, but we didn't realize how *very* dangerous. We have never discussed his work at home, but, of course, there is gossip at school, sometimes rather cruel about the business and that rubbing out of Denz who used to live here.'

'I remember Denzil,' Ralph said. 'He had an attic flat, didn't he?'

'Unfortunately, he failed to maintain a happy relationship with Daddy. There are big stresses in the business world, aren't there? Perhaps your work is the same, Mr Ember, so your children, if you have any, might get some slagging off at school from other kids, and it's necessary to smack such very hard in the gob, flat back of the hand, not fist, in case of bashing out teeth which can get stuck in your knuckles, plus trouble with the management and parents. The human bite is one of the most toxic, so to get somebody's tooth or teeth fixed into your skin even for a short while can bring infection. But if nuisances get a good swipe across the chops or maybe two swipes, from left to right and then back, they shut up, the yellow, ninny prats. Luckily, blood doesn't show too badly on blue blazers. Are you visiting now because of work, Mr Ember?'

'Your daddy and I have known each other for many years,' Ralph replied.

The den room had a massive, old-style partner's desk with what looked like some of Matilda's school books on it; a suite in red leather – oddly, Ralph had red leather furniture himself at Low Pastures – a large safe and a bookcase with hard- and paperbacked volumes in it. There were art portraits on the walls, including one of a plumpish woman who seemed as if she was from several centuries back. Ember got the idea from somewhere that she might be Dutch. She wore a red, inverted flower-pot-type hat which Ralph thought might have been common in Holland at the time, flower pots being plentiful because of the daffodil crop. In the hall hung pre-Raphaelite paintings of thinner women in bright clothes. Manse greatly favoured the pre-Raphaelites. Some of his collection would be genuine, most probably. He went to auctions and had plenty of funds.

But Shale had art from many different periods and Matilda, sitting under a surreal catastrophe of super-bright squares, circles, semi-circles, rectangles and zebras' striped heads, said, 'Why, I hope this is a friendliness visit, not just work. Mr Ember, if it's only work and the work, like Daddy's, is dangerous, as shown in the gunnery against Naomi and Laurent, an error, then there are certain results. I've been trying to decide whether if it's only work this means there is twice as much of such work because there are two of you, and therefore twice as much risk; or only half as much work and therefore only half as much risk because the work has to be divided into two, half for each of you.'

Ralph saw this was a clever girl. She could get to the line of thinking behind her daddy's plans without even knowing about the plans. Yes, Ralph and Manse would split the work on Waverton between action (by Ralph) and alibi (by Manse). But there would also be twice as much because, as well as Waverton (by Ralph) there would eventually be that other one, selected (by Ralph) but seen off (by Shale). Ember reckoned Matilda would end up with top marks at the Harvard Business School a few years from now. He guessed she had formed her ideas independently and without help from her daddy. Ralph felt pretty certain

Manse wouldn't have discussed with his daughter the strangers on a train plan for the elimination of Waverton.

'When the shooting happened I was in the back of the Jag with Laurent, you know, Mr Ember,' Matilda said.

'Yes,' Ralph replied.

'In a way he shielded me,' she said.

'Yes,' Ralph said.

'Some people thought an incident of this kind would have an effect on me, referred to by medics within my hearing as deleterious, if you know that word, which I looked up, meaning not too good. This would be because of the broken glass and the noise and the blood and fragments on my clothes and face and in my hair. I got down to the floor quicker than Laurent. Or perhaps he stayed upright deliberately to protect me.'

'Yes,' Ralph replied.

'I had to have a counsellor,' Matilda said. 'This was recommended. I didn't mind.'

'That can often be a help, I believe,' Ralph said.

'I told her the effect on me was I'd make sure I always had a back seat in any car and, if possible, with someone else alongside me. That is, until I'm driving myself, obviously.'

'Yes,' Ralph replied.

FIVE

Shale came back with the refreshments on a tray. 'Matty's going to remain here and complete her homework, Ralph.' He gave her a glass of squash and said to Ember, 'We'll withdraw into the withdrawing room, shall we, Ralph?' His snub face was merry and snubbier than ever to back up the quip.

This was what Ralph meant when he thought of Manse as having some self-awareness. He seemed to realize that if he'd said, 'We'll go into the drawing room, shall we, Ralph?' it would sound highfalutin and corny, so he hatched a little, cumbersome joke. Just the same, this other part of the rectory had obviously been furnished and decorated as a drawing room – heavy red and gold flock wallpaper, two big settees in brown leather facing each other, four easy chairs, also in brown leather, a chiffonier in mahogany, a round, rosewood table, and light blue rugs on the sanded and varnished floorboards

Four pistols and shoulder holsters were laid out on the lovely rosewood table. The weapons glinted mischievously under the lights. Guns didn't show wear, so there was no knowing at this stage whether they had a history, but to Ralph they looked unused. Certainly the holsters seemed new. Shale ignored the armament and pointed Ralph towards one of the settees. He'd kept the tray. On it were two glasses, a corkscrew and a bottle of white wine in an ice bucket. Manse went and opened the bottle and filled the glasses. He passed one to Ralph, then sat down opposite him with the other.

'Did I have it right about the dancer the other night?' Ralph asked.

'Typically quick of you, Ralph. Yes, that was Waverton. He came close to show he got no cause to expect any hate from me. No, to *pretend* he got no cause to expect any hate from me. The jigging nearly toe-to-toe with us is him saying he's having a great, carefree time and there's nothing at the Agincourt to worry and/or scare him. This he've got very fucking wrong twice over: *I'm* there and so are you.'

The wine was a Sauvignon Blanc and Ralph recognized what the trade called the 'gunflint' smoky smell off it. Maybe the pistols nearby added something to the gunflint bouquet. A classy drink. He'd want to get at least ninety pounds a bottle for it if served by the glass at the Monty. Manse really tried hard not to be a peasant. Maybe he knew something about wine as well as art.

'I notice you noticing the weaponry, Ralph.'

'It's very open, very much on view.'

'I wanted to display a selection like, properly arranged.'

'Nobody could fail to see the guns.'

'Ah, you're thinking of Matty, I expect, wondering if she might spot them, be shocked, upset.'

'But perhaps the drawing room is out of bounds to her,' Ember replied.

'This is a family home, Ralph. The family is reduced as to numbers, yes, but those who survive got to have a total run of the property or the family home wouldn't be a family home, would it?'

'That's certainly a point, Manse.'

'Matilda got an attitude to firearms which is what you'd expect when someone's been on the end of a salvo, with a stepmother and brother riddled and slumped in a damaged top-of-the-range car on account of that same blundering salvo. She knows that salvo should of taken her daddy, not shared out between Naomi and Laurent who got no roles as targets. Them bullets had Daddy's name on them but they got misdelivered. She knows her daddy is still alive and totally unriddled, ditto herself, and there might be another try on him. So, she figures if there's more gunfire ready for her daddy any day, then her daddy got to have his own gunfire ready to stop that other gunfire getting at him. There's a kind of pattern to it, isn't there, Ralph?

'She got to think that if her daddy gets salvoed next time she'll be on her own, not in this much-loved rectory with all its fine memories of her life here, but forced to go off to

some municipal general home for orphans where there'd be
no art to speak of. Or her mother, Sybil, might say, OK, Matty
could come to her and her partner, but we already seen what
Sybil thinks about children – that it's smart to get a lot of
distance between her and them, if possible into a different
country. And then, in any case, what's this partner like? Is he
thinking he'd better offer this pretty girl child plentiful regular
attention and comfort because of what she been through and
having to live in North Wales? You know what I mean? This
could be a traffic warden or a surgeon. Do you think we can
trust that sort? I heard there's a movie and a book about this
type of thing – the man getting to the young daughter by joining
up with the mother.'

'*Lolita*,' Ember replied, 'by Nabokov.'

'Probably he'd need a foreign name to write about such
shabby sex.'

'He was born in Russia but became American.'

'There you are then,' Shale said. 'I would of bet on that. And
then them municipal homes. What do we hear about what goes
on in some of them? Matty reads the papers, watches the news,
and she knows the best answer re keeping things as they are
now and as they should be, is armament. It's only logical, isn't
it, Ralph? Maybe you already got your own armament at home
or in the club. This would be absolutely understandable. You
got a very considerable person to safeguard – you! I think of
them letters in the press, by Ralph W. Ember, to do with heavy
topics, especially the environment.'

'Well, yes.'

'But such a personal gun don't fit the pattern, as referred to
previous. It don't fit the S.O.A.T., the strangers on a train, policy.
There got to be no traceability of a weapon, and no possibility
of traceability of a weapon, so newness and purchase from an
experienced and trusted dealer is the absolute requirement.'

'But there are *four* guns, Manse. That's a lot for self-defence,
isn't it?'

'Four, are there?'

'Well, you can see them there – four. As you said, a selection.'

'Yes, it could be four. Matty's a very practical child.'

'In which regard, Manse?'

'If she saw them four there she'd realize guns can jam sometimes. A reserve might be needed.'

'Yes, but four, Manse?'

'Matilda knows I'm someone who gets moods – like preferring this to that one day, and then not much later preferring that to this. No real reason for it, just inclinations. Whims. Perhaps everyone's a bit like this – temperamental. That's how it was with them girls she might of mentioned to you in the den, Lowri, Patricia, Carmel. All very lovely in their ways, and Carmel extremely well up on the porcelain and Adolf's struggle, but me getting a special satisfaction from one of them for anything up to six weeks or even a couple of months, really settled, steady. Then somehow a change needed. Imposs to explain. The particular girl might of been behaving like always, sweet, kindly, warm, ever-ready, yet along comes this urge – this unbelievably powerful urge – this urgent urge, you might call it – this comes along and I have to put her aside for a while and move on to one of the others. As I hope Matty said, strictly never more than one at a time. I got no interest in multi-romps, threesomes, foursomes, Ralph, a tit-and-arse glut. That would be deeply immoderate and an insult to the girls concerned. I wouldn't call myself a feminist, Ralph, but they got to have a certain quantity of respect or where are we? Anyway, it could be the same with the weaponry. I might take a strong fancy to, say, a Smith and Wesson one day, an excellent pistol, but, then, not long after a Walther, or a Browning. They all got their special features, Ralph, like them girls.'

'But they are laid out for *me,* aren't they, Manse, not *you,* The guns, I mean, not the girls,' Ember replied.

'Matty might not realize that. But who can tell? She speaks about friendship, wants a true friendship between you and me. Underneath that word, "friendship", though might be a more serious thought than what she calls "a chat". She could mean a gun friendship, so she'd decide I must be taking care of your tastes as well as mine re the small arms.

'Or then again, Ralph, if grave trouble started here, in the rectory – an attack by follow-up bastards to the jinxed Jag event, Matty might – Matty *would* – yes, she would want a piece for herself, I think. She's young for an automatic, yes, but we're talking about a hellish crisis – no time for birth certificates. That's how she is, she don't like weakness. She was first one down on the floor in the Jag. Why? Not fear, but because she got a kind of soldier's instinct. She can smell the battle before it happens and so she's ready to take cover and then fight back, if only she'd had something to fight back with, but simply a haversack for her school books on that terrible occasion.'

Ralph was conscious of some very elegant, sneaky salesmanship under way. The fact that verbs and other fiddly bits of sentence-making gave Manse chronic, merciless trouble didn't signify Manse lacked brain-power: Matilda got at least some of her sharpness from her daddyo. There even seemed to be a kind of telepathic link between their minds. Manse Shale knew how to manage a situation.

Consider the guns, for instance, nicely presented by him like *nouveau cuisine*. Ralph knew he was supposed to make his choice, one or two, in case of the jamming possibility already mentioned. But never mind the various attributes of the weapons, Ralph felt it was the *timing* of the choice that really mattered. He was being asked to pick his gun, or guns, before the need to kill Waverton had been proved, or fractionally proved.

Ralph had come here tonight to discuss the murder script in a balanced, thorough style and, most important, to be offered good evidence that it *was* Waverton from inside Manse's firm who gave the geography for a school-run interception. There'd been no talk along those lines so far, only a case history of Matilda as to guns: her wise, juvenile, hard-headed respect for them.

Wrapped up in that was the unspoken invitation for Ralph to follow his tastes, his 'moods', and act on this school kid's very practical endorsement of firearms, as reported by Daddyo, and kit himself out with one he fancied. Or two he fancied. If, or when, he did that he would be committing himself to the SOAT programme, of course. Yes, timing. Get the gun/guns first and then decide, like one of those urgent urges, that this gun, these guns, ought to be used, or what the hell was a gun, or guns, *for*?

Ralph guessed that a leap of phoney logic, non-logic, in fact, was sure to arrive next. It would suggest that since the gun or

guns had to be put to work, put it or them to work on Waverton.
And if Ralph had the cheek to ask whether Waverton definitely
deserved it, Manse would probably reply, with a pitying smile
at Ember's blindness and stupidity, that, obviously, the bastard,
Waverton, had flagrantly danced close to him and Ralph at the
Agincourt, hoping to show he had no reason to feel any guilt
over the Jaguar tragedy because he did, in fact, have a very
solid reason to feel guilt over the Jaguar tragedy, namely, he'd
supplied the itinerary. Manse would see the invasive dancing
as a brazen, disgraceful bluff, but not a bluff with the least
chance of convincing him. Most likely he would consider the
dancing as not only an insult to himself but also to the Agincourt
Hotel and to the glorious British history typified in that name,
Agincourt, and to longbows.

Manse spoke off-handedly now, matter-of-factly, lolling back
slightly with his drink on the settee: 'Naturally, Ralph, I had
to realize that you might think this . . . this . . . this, well, what's
the word . . . you might think this concept . . . yes, concept
– it's an unusual word for me, admitted, but yes, this concept,
you might consider this concept a total trap.'

'Which concept, Manse?'

'The Waverton death concept.'

'But a trap, how?'

'We're business people, Ralph,' Shale replied.

'Certainly.'

'I think of Karl Marx.'

'In which aspect, Manse?'

'I believe Karl Marx said one capitalist company would
always try to destroy any rival. It had to. It was its nature;
capitalism's absolute, basic rule. This is why I said a trap.'

'I don't understand, Manse.'

'You're a business, Ralph. I'm a business. Marx would say
we were bound to try to trample each other under, although in
some way we're mates, but that matiness nothing like as strong
as the pressures of business sink-or-swim.'

'Oh, Marx, we don't take much notice of him, not since the
Wall came down, surely, Manse,' Ember said.

'I got to think of things like *you* think of things, Ralph.'

This was something else to piss Ember off vastly – Shale

talking as though he had a mind capable of the same level of thought as Ralph. Manse might be smart and clever, but that was different from intellect and Ralph considered Manse couldn't get anywhere near him for intellect. He must be too self-obsessed to realize what an insult he'd just delivered. But Ralph considered Shale ought at least to have the sense not to speak such a slur aloud, even if in his profound vanity he believed it.

Good God, didn't this twirp realize that a plaque had been fixed to one of the perimeter gates at Low Pasture, by a previous owner – definitely not 'Caring'– with an unquestionably genuine Latin inscription on it. Ralph often gave the plaque a rub-over and checked it was still securely attached. Classical languages he doted on. He didn't understand them but delighted in their durability and survival, despite other lingoes coming along and trying to push them under with slang such as 'fit' and 'leg-over'. Most probably in one of those far-back periods most of the conversation in Low Pastures would have been in Latin, to prove the residents had education and refinement, though not the servants. If Ralph had been around then, he would have made certain he spoke Latin more or less always.

This rectory wouldn't have such a learned plaque. He'd described it to himself just now as 'ordinary' and he still believed that. Ralph guessed there wouldn't be more than seven bedrooms to the Old Rectory, perhaps only six, and you could hardly think of its little areas of garden as grounds – no paddocks or stables as at Low Pastures. The rectory stood in a city suburb and so had only a restricted setting: no vistas that took in great slabs of countryside and, eventually, the sea, as at Low Pastures. There was the rectory's tree-lined, curved, gravelled drive which admittedly gave the rectory some distance from the busy road – Ralph wanted to be fair – but nothing could quell traffic noise. At Low Pastures you might hear a fox bark or rooks cawing but that would be all – nature. Ember was enthusiastically in favour of nature, but he knew Manse regarded it as a menace, liable to take over everything if not severely and constantly hacked back. Although the sea might not be visible from the Old Rectory, Manse went pretty often to the coast to check on possible beach-creep by the waves, and he worried constantly about erosion of cliffs.

'As *I* think of things? In which regard, Manse?' Ember replied.

'In which regard as to what?'

'My thinking and you sort of attempting to re-run it.'

'I have to imagine if I was you, Ralph, and you came along – you being me in this sort of changed situation – yes, if you being me came along to me, being you, and said you'd like me, being you, to do a kill for me, being you, I might have to wonder – I being you, of course – I'd have to wonder whether you – that is actually me – whether you was scheming to get me into a situation where I – that is, you – could be scuppered.'

Shale put this forward in a slow, gentle voice, as if to recognize it might be difficult for someone like Ralph to follow the flow of what was being said; and so Manse would considerately keep the demands on Ember's attention at a minimum. Ralph's anger swelled, in his view, justified anger, 'righteous anger', as it might be termed in some religions. He would have loved to take a serrated knife to this fucking stately fat brown leather fucking furniture, and take a not necessarily very big hammer to some of the art on the walls in here, and possibly genuine originals; or not just some of it, all of it. They talked of pictures going 'under the hammer' at auctions, didn't they? No need for an auction. But why was he short of a hammer?

'And what's the answer when you do your fantasy reversal of roles, Manse?' Ember replied, showing a warm, good-humoured smile at the Shale tangled gibberish. Ralph secretly clawed away at the cushion under him with the fingers of his free hand to assess the thickness of the leather and estimate the degree of maddened knife force needed to shred this cow pelt. Why the hell had he come here? What was he doing, staying on meekly in this dud property?

Ralph regarded the rectory as a totally adequate depot for one of the big Victorian families before satisfactory condoms or the pill, or TV as a distraction, but that was as much as you could say about it. In fact, Ralph wouldn't say *anything* about it to Manse – wouldn't ever indicate in words or behaviour that Ember regarded it as a step down to come to the Old Rectory. When Ralph considered what a half-educated entity Manse basically was, it had to be seen as splendid, as marvellous, that he'd created a business able to supply him with the cost, even for a 'home' like this. Shale and Matilda lived here on their own now.

As Matilda had reminded him, there was a flat on the top storey, occupied for a while by Denzil Lake, Manse's former chauffeur and bodyguard, whose face became permanently slightly aslant through talking to Shale in the back of the Jag while looking ahead. But Denz had been executed in very necessary circumstances lately[2] and although after some time Manse had taken on a replacement driver/minder, this one had a family house and didn't require the flat. Obviously, it was during the spell between chauffeurs that Naomi, Manse's second wife, did the school run that bad day. Shale's first wife, Sybil, was shacked up somewhere in North Wales, Manse had said, with a partner he thought was 'a heart surgeon, or roofer or traffic warden or broker', and he'd earnestly prefer she stayed there.

'What I mean, then, to put it straight as straight, Ralph, which I always aim to do, but especially in my own accommodation, it being of a religious pedigree – what I mean is, I come to you, Ralph Ember, and ask you to see off someone I think is an enemy of mine, a traitor, and I promise to do the same for you if you need an enemy took out in the future. But suppose I see the chance to get rid of two problem people, not one – Waverton and you, Ralph, you not being an enemy in the Waverton fashion, clearly, but an enemy in the Karl Marx sense just as clearly – someone who is bound to try to destroy me because that's something built in to business, into capitalism: annihilate all competition, or it will annihilate you. So, you goes ahead and does Waverton and I'm one of the first the police want to see following discovery of the body because we was close business colleagues and might have had, say, a money squabble, or a woman squabble, or a leadership squabble. But me, knowing where and when Waverton would be done, is a long way off at that precise juncture accompanied by plenty of pure-as-pure people who can honestly, uncontradictably, say I

[2] See *I Am Gold*

was with them in a restaurant or a regatta or a Buckingham Palace garden party. The police – stymied.

'But you might worry, Ralph, that when I'm in their question-and-answer room, I might mention that Waverton, an esteemed staffer, had told me in super-confidence that he was afraid Ralph Ember had some kind of serious territory dispute with him and seemed very threatening. You might also, Ralph, worry that I would scatter some clues here and there and findable by the police to get you in the frame for this death. As I said, scuppered.

'I want to describe this with the full twists and turns now because I got to admit you could be thinking like this, Ralph, and I want to say that, although I could understand them feelings and doubts it would never be like this in reality.'

'Some big thinker declared humankind cannot bear very much reality,' Ralph said. He needed a break from the stifling monologue.

'But there's a hell of a lot of it about,' Shale replied.

'What?'

'Reality. I got to take account of it, Ralph. I feel I should bring these possible worries of yours out into the open so I can deal with them head-on, crush them, kill them, also in the open. Ralph, I would *never, never* use that kind of filthy trap against you, regardless of Karl Marx.'

Ralph went beyond a smile now, and gave a large, humane, brilliantly comradely laugh. He recovered his fingers from the superior soft leather. He spoke almost off-handedly, unemphatically as if what he had to say hardly required saying at all, it was so obviously the truth: 'No, no need to fantasize, Manse. And no need to kowtow to the gospel of dear Karl. I'm here to discuss the reality of the Waverton operation, not to take fright at alarmist dreams or worn-out political theory.'

'Thank you, Ralph. Thank you, thank you.'

'I believe it can be said, Manse, that over the years we have established a business relationship of abiding mutual trust and respect.'

'Yes, Ralph, oh, yes.'

Ember had, of course, thought about the possibility of being deliberately led into disaster by a shitty Shale manoeuvre.

But he hated the notion that Manse might be observant enough to detect this suspicion in Ralph. All right, Ember would admit Shale was surprisingly clever, but not *that* surprisingly clever. He must be put in his place and made to feel deeply wrong. And so Ralph had to pretend with blazing sincerity to Manse and, more significantly, to himself, that this suspicion *never, never* existed. The Waverton project remained powerfully ongoing.

This didn't mean they should hobnob in each other's properties, though. He *had* allowed Manse to enter Low Pastures once but he didn't think it would be suitable to make this a recurring matter, despite the child's suggestion. Manse probably would never feel OK socially in a grand, prestige dwelling like Low Pastures, with its lovely, wide staircase, exposed stone walls and undoubted Latin on a gate. In any case, if they went through with the destruction of Waverton as well as someone not yet nominated by Ralph, it wouldn't be wise to have a lot of pre-get-togethers. Even dropping in like this tonight might bring future risks if someone saw Ralph's car entering the drive.

Clearly they could not be fully like the strangers on a train, because they were *not* strangers. But the contact between them should be minimal, otherwise the Manse swap-plot became useless. There would be evidence of a conspiracy.

One of the things that surprised some people when considering a bit of rough like Manse was that he knew so much about art and liked so many types of painting, but especially the pre-Raphaelites. Those artists had a brotherhood, and Manse fancied belonging to something like that, fucking the models interchangeably. Plenty of pictures hung in the hall of the rectory, but Ralph thought they must be prints only. It would be mad to have the valuable stuff so near the front door and at the end of a winding drive, which meant nobody from the street could see a break-in and subsequent exit with the takings.

When Ralph had arrived here tonight Shale and Matilda would have led on into the house immediately but Ralph paused to look at several of the works and dollop out some greasy praise about perspective, brushwork and such. It didn't matter if they were fakes. In fact, it might be best if they *were* fakes. In a strange fashion this might be a plus for Manse. Ralph would hate him to feel troubled and lowly at having the owner of a country estate on his minor property and making comparisons, Low Pastures being anything but lowly. Ralph's appreciation act in the hall had been intended to help Manse feel some temporary superiority over Ember, particularly if Ralph showed himself fooled by production-line copies. Ralph loathed snobbery and would do almost anything to save a yobbish, jumped-up jerk like Shale from it.

SIX

'Those eyes,' she said, 'those animal-like eyes, ferrety.'

'Manse's?'

'I haven't spoken about this before – too vague. An impression only? I thought the memory would fade. It hasn't. More than a week and it hasn't.'

'At the Agincourt?'

'You noticed?'

'Like a message: "Don't dance so close."'

'Yes, but more than that.'

'Oh, yes, yes, more than that,' Waverton said.

'But *you* haven't spoken about it, either.'

'Didn't want to alarm you. Like you said, it's vague, could be just an impression, Rose.'

'But enough to alarm me? Those two spotted it as well?'

'Which two?'

'Harpur and Iles, though Iles hadn't fully recovered from being dumped by Pinkerton. In case Iles broke down again from sorrow Harpur took him home soon afterwards, didn't he?' Rose said.

'Harpur does manage him.'

'I heard Harpur was having it off with Mrs Iles for a while. That establishes a fine bond between two men, doesn't it?' Rose at the wheel, they were driving to the city swimming baths to watch their daughter compete freestyle in the annual inter-schools gala.

Frank Waverton said, 'I think Shale believes I laid the trail to Naomi and the boy. No, no – laid the trail to *Manse*, but we get a changed driver and a mess up by the gunman.'

'Oh, hell,' she said, 'that could be bloody awkward.'

'And he might wonder whether there'll be another go at him, with me offering guidance again.'

'Oh, hell.' Rose found she couldn't ask the obvious question: *Did* you lay the trail? That would treat it as at least a possibility, and the idea sickened her. Horribly difficult moments in her marriage would arrive suddenly like this occasionally. Her life wasn't simple. She went quiet, pretended to be preoccupied with the driving, but really thinking hard. As part of that she recalled the final scenes of *Godfather 1*. Kay Corleone asks her Mafia husband, Michael, and keeps asking, whether he ordered the murder of his own brother-in-law. Eventually, Michael agrees to answer and says, 'No.' She's hugely relieved. But the audience knows he's an out-and-out, disgusting, professional liar. We saw him organize the garotting. Rose couldn't bear the notion that she might force Frank into lying. But she couldn't bear the notion, either, that he wouldn't lie, and admit he'd helped set up the ambush.

Rose often found herself running bits of the first two *Godfather* films in her head. The movies displayed the grim, painful dilemmas of a law-abiding woman married into a family and business society of violent career male villains. It brought big problems. Rose knew something about them.

But Frank wasn't Michael Corleone and wasn't dim either. She glanced at him in the passenger seat of the Merc. He gave what seemed to her something between a grin and a wince. Perhaps he recognized her difficulties and sympathized – so, the grin. Or was he hurt to see Rose feared she might dig out a horrifying truth – so, the wince? There were moments like these now when she couldn't read Frank. And he didn't seem able to read her, either. Perhaps in what had become a shadowy relationship it was always going to be like this at times of unexpected crisis – distance, incomprehension, as with Kay and Michael.

Frank said, 'Maybe at the Agincourt he considered I was putting on a happy show to conceal guilt and shame. That would enrage him. Turn his eyes ferrety.'

'And Ember was there with him. How does Ralph come into all this?'

'Not clear. But they're sort of friends.'

'Which sort?'

'Exactly,' Frank said.

'What does that mean?'

'They're ordered by Iles to be friends.'

'Ordered?'

'Iles demands peace on the streets. As long as they provide

it – no turf battles – he'll let them run their businesses serenely and side by side.'

'But has he got the authority to do that? It's blind-eyeing king-size crookedness.'

'Iles does it. Gets away with it.'

'So far,' she said.

'So far. There's a well-informed, very respectable lobby in favour of legalization. Perhaps that's useful for him.'

'The Jag deaths must have shaken that Iles–Shale–Ember arrangement.'

'Of course. But it survives.'

'How?'

'You don't ask whether Shale might be right to hate and hunt me, Rose,' Frank replied, speaking very slowly, as though forcing himself.

'Hate and hunt you for helping get his wife and son killed, and for endangering that splendid commercial co-existence?'

'Yes.'

'Of course I don't ask,' she said.

'You dread the possible answer?'

'I *know* the answer.'

'How can you know?'

'I know *you*,' she said. Naturally, Rose recognized this was not completely true, maybe not even substantially true, but how she would have liked it to be. Wives should be able to say that kind of thing to their husbands straight off. Well, she did say it to her husband straight off, but only to smokescreen her doubts. 'I know you couldn't do something like that.' Yes, that was how she would have liked it to be, the certainty, absolute, sweeping and instant. No go, though.

'Thanks, Rose.'

The terrible error of the shooting confused things for her. In some ways helping in the slaughter of Naomi and Laurent had been an accident, only the gunman to blame. Would aiding in the intended wipeout of Manse have been comparatively reasonable; most probably commercial rivalry gone too far? But obviously – and obviously again – Shale might not think so. He would see it as treachery.

*   *   *

Watching their daughter splash and trundle-crawl her way to victories in her heats and finals, Rose decided Olive had the power but seemed very short on style. Although at the moment that was to do with her swimming, the same could be said about Olive's approach to life in general. Did it matter? Not much, in Rose's view. Olive had the essentials. All they needed was some polish. A good, settled home life could help with this. She and Frank could – would – supply it for as long and as well as they could. This was the kind of consideration that tied Rose into the marriage, regardless. And possibly tied him in, too. Rose needed him safe, and would try to make sure he was.

She thought about Shale's daughter and what she had been through. How had it affected her? How did it affect her now? Appalling mischance or not, was Frank in part responsible for this, and for the deaths? Rose still longed to push that question out of sight. 'Olive's going to be a little while,' she said. 'Let's go to the car now. I want to fuck.'

'There are lights over the car park, possible CCTV.'

'So they'll get a good shot of your bum. But it's reasonably anon, isn't it?'

SEVEN

Harpur saw the Wavertons suddenly stand and leave their seats near the shallow end of the pool and make their way towards the exit, although the gala hadn't formally finished yet. Of the two, she seemed to move more urgently. Harpur waited briefly and then went after them. It was a discussion this morning with Iles that brought Harpur to the swimming baths, watching the Wavertons now.

Although Waverton had never been charged with anything, the Drugs Squad kept a file on him and Harpur learned his address and that he was married to Rose, aged 33, with a twelve-year-old daughter, Olive, at the same comprehensive school as Harpur's daughters. Harpur recognized Rose as Waverton's partner at the Agincourt dancing.

If he wanted to stay unobserved Harpur would have to be careful. He didn't really rate as a gumshoe. He had too much bulk and couldn't blend neatly into his surrounds. To quite a degree, he *was* his surrounds. He had nothing spectral about him. Some said he looked like a fair-haired Rocky Marciano, undefeated world heavyweight boxing champion in the 1950s. The Wavertons would identify Harpur, of course. He appeared now and then on local TV news programmes giving the police account of some crime, or some conviction. In any case, it would be a basic requirement for someone in Frank Waverton's career to know at least by sight the top local police.

And there had been the Agincourt and the attention Iles brought to both of them by his gaudy period of international mourning for *Madame Butterfly*. Several pieces of music had the power to upset the ACC in this way, and Harpur always kept alert when with him at parties and so on in case Iles chose to perform one of these numbers and wring his considerable soul. Harpur felt he must be very ready immediately after the rendering to give comfort and reassurance and to wipe him down. Obviously, it was best, if possible, to persuade Iles not to sing, especially at very select occasions, such as, say, a civic reception for the Queen and Prince Philip, or the Home Secretary. Iles could be very stubborn, though, and would usually ignore these pleas. 'I will not be censored,' he'd shouted once at Harpur. 'Freedom of expression is my totem.'

The First World War song, 'There's a silver lining, through the dark clouds shining,' could melt Iles, and his voice would take on the thin, sad, quivering tone of a mouth organ in the Great War trenches. Another composition that made him desolate was 'The minstrel boy to the war is gone, In the ranks of death you'll find him.' The kid had his father's sword and a harp. The second verse started 'The Minstrel fell,' and Iles used to topple himself over as if devastated by shrapnel when he reached this, but on the ground mimicked tearing the harp's 'cords asunder', as in the song, so no enemy could play one of their own unholy, polluting tunes on it. After one of these casualty episodes, Iles had explained to Harpur, 'Nowadays, Col, someone would tell him to take a Kalashnikov into the battle not a fucking harp.'

Iles always recovered fairly quickly from songster laments. The morning following the Agincourt Butterfly crisis, he had said, 'The dancing, Col.'

'Last night? Too funky and up-to-the-minute for me. Or is funky itself out-of-date now? I'll ask my daughters. I prefer the veleta.'

'I'd like you to think of Manse,' Iles had replied.

'Sitting with Ralph Ember, watching.'

'Watching with unusual intentness, would you say?'

'I've never seen them watching dancing before, so I don't know if they were unusually intent. Is there an intentness norm for watching dancing?'

'And their intentness developing how, Harpur?'

'Developing in what sense, sir?'

'In the sense of developing,' Iles replied. 'Attitude.'

'To?'

'Oh, yes, to.'

Harpur and Iles had been talking in the ACC's office suite at headquarters, two rooms, one occupied by a large conference table and a dozen straight-backed chairs, the other with easy chairs, a work station and a tiltable cheval mirror so he could check his appearance selectively – selectively meaning he was able to avoid any reflection of his Adam's apple, which he considered unforgivably knotty. Iles paced. Harpur had one of the armchairs. Iles liked pacing, an unhurried, musing lope. Harpur reckoned today's was a lope with big significance. He'd thought about loping himself, but realized they might get into an awkward congestion at some point. He stayed put. Iles had on one of his London custom-made grey, double-breasted, three-piece suits, mauve-striped shirt, plain mauve tie in what he called a 'Windsor knot', a plump, inverted triangle fashion set by Edward VIII when Prince of Wales. It was said to have sexual relevance. 'Attitude towards the Wavertons, Col. They were dancing more or less into Shale's and Ember's laps.'

'I took it as a kind of thank you,' Harpur had said, 'like a military march-past, to honour some admiral of the fleet.'

'Did you? Did you, Col? How generous.'

'Ralph or Manse paying for the night on rotation. People would want to show they're having a lovely time and are grateful. Perhaps they'd try to express that in their own style – say, dancing. This would be so, although they'd been very genuinely moved, as we all were, by your touching remembrance of *Madame Butterfly*. They'd wish to prove that this spell of pain, extremely valid though it definitely was, had ended now and the jollifications, as catered for by Ralph or Manse, could resume. Dance is such a positive, isn't it, sir? A community expression, in this case the Shale and Ember combined community. Think of John Travolta.'

Iles was on his way to the far end of the conference room and had spoken over his shoulder. 'A stratagem, Col. A ploy.'

'In which particular, sir?'

Iles turned back. 'Manse wasn't fooled by it. Oh no! Did you see his eyes?'

'Manse has had some suffering,' Harpur replied.

'He saw what Waverton was trying to do.'

'What was that, sir?'

'I'd say Waverton knows that Manse has him in mind,' Iles said.

'In mind in which respect?'

'Those eyes, they're directed at Waverton and what are they telling us, Col?'

'Eyes can certainly express a lot. They say TV acting is all about eyes – no need to bellow and arm-wave to reach the back row of the stalls. I notice the eyes in that soap, *EastEnders*. The eyes have a hell of a lot to say for themselves.'

'Those eyes remark very tersely to Waverton, "I've got you marked, mate, and don't imagine that if you do a ninety seconds' jig in my and Ralph's personal space this puts everything right; some matters have to be answered for, have to be suffered for."'

'Were Ralph Ember's eyes tersing the same sort of message to Waverton?'

'Ralph can measure a situation long-term, Col. Remember his letters to the press about our environment. He's looking far, far ahead.'

'Exactly which situation do you have in mind, sir?'

'Oh, yes,' Iles replied. 'That accounts for their closeness.'

'Sitting together at the Agincourt?'

'Beyond this, Harpur. You, at your rank, are not accustomed to looking into that beyond. I don't blame you in the least. It is the nature of things, given your qualities. If you ever got to staff college, which, obviously, you won't, not with clothes and a haircut like that, but if you did you would be made familiar with phrases such as "think width", "penetrate the beyond", "be not anchored in the everyday, the immediate, the superficial, escape the merely mechanical, the banausic."'

'Ban the banausic! This would be a challenge, sir.'

'It would be and you'd probably make a total fuck-up of it.'

'I might practise thinking width.'

'What Ralph understands is that Waverton and Waverton's malign, secret associates have failed once,' Iles replied. 'This does not mean they will abandon their filthy project. They had everything right except the personnel – not Manse himself but his wife and child. They will want to correct. They will come again. And this time they might do what they meant to do previously, get Manse. Ralph recognizes this. Ralph fears this. It would bring perilous imbalance to the city. It would bring in outside traders who want Manse's firm and who would not be interested in the kind of mature concordat that exists now between Ralph's and Shale's businesses. Having rid the scene of Manse they would almost certainly try to take over Ember's companies as well. This is why I referred to Ralph as an embodiment of long-term thought.'

'Would that thought have width as well as length?'

'Ralph and Manse will seek to look after each other,' Iles replied. 'There are bonds.'

Harpur, of course, recognized that Iles's guesses often turned out right, and so Harpur was at the city swimming bath now watching an inter-schools' gala – or watching the Wavertons watching an inter-schools' gala – and following them at a tactical distance when they left. He'd thought he could work out from the pattern of their clapping and yelling during the races the child they supported: a girl in her pre-teens, not too graceful in the water, but strong and dogged, a winner in all her crawl events for John Locke Comprehensive School: Olive. Harpur's daughters preferred judo to swimming and weren't at the gala tonight.

Harpur's belief that Iles could foresee meant that marginally more often than not – say 60 per cent to 40 per cent – if he felt like interpreting a situation he would get it correct, almost regardless of evidence one way or the other. For instance, a pair danced near to Ember and Shale and therefore Iles would say the man must be part responsible for the death of Naomi and Laurent Shale, and could be lining up an attempt on Manse, to correct the earlier botched one. Was this a mad bit of theorizing? If it had come from anyone else Harpur would have thought so and instantly dismissed it. But Iles could prophesy. Harpur had decided to put a discreet spell of surveillance on Waverton. Because he wouldn't have been able to offer a credible, sane briefing on this operation to any of his detective staff, he'd do it himself.

He followed them into the baths' car park. They walked to the Mercedes Harpur had tailed here earlier from their home. Waverton unlocked the doors and they climbed in – climbed into the back. Harpur wondered what the ACC would have divined from this, and from the seeming eagerness of Rose to get to the vehicle. The car park was well lit, and probably had CCTV. Just the same, they were plainly ready to accept the risk. Was Rose depressed and uncertain about something, and in need of an immediate act of reassurance on the state of the relationship with Frank? A back-seat get together might be intended to deliver this reassurance, and to hell with lights and cameras.

Harpur went to his own car. He didn't fancy hanging about near the Mercedes. Naturally, he would acknowledge that voyeurism could be regarded as a kind of community celebration, the sharing in a joyful, possibly fruitful carry-on; but he didn't much go for it, all the same. He thought he would feel excluded, an outsider, and this must be especially so if he were skulking at the window of a high-grade car, such as a newish Mercedes. There'd be a sort of deprived urchin quality to such behaviour. This didn't necessarily mean that Harpur wanted to be invited in to make up a threesome, just that he had little curiosity about community fondnesses. There were people about who enjoyed being watched and/or watching, in car parks, lay-bys, back lanes. An official term had been invented: dogging. Not to Harpur's taste, though, or not yet. And he didn't think the Wavertons' were motivated like that, either. They'd responded to a sudden need, especially Rose.

He liked her go-get spirit; the positive reasoning that lay behind this extra-mural love session. She would probably argue that if their marriage had troubles, doubts, disturbing – possibly sinister – puzzles, the best remedy was good sex, regardless of location.

Iles, if told, would certainly want details that Harpur couldn't provide: which side of the car was her head; would it be liable to bang against the metal Mercedes shell at crux moments, or crux minutes, possibly concussing her; what, if any, noises – and above all, speech; which garments discarded; any instances of Rose's feet hitting the hazard switch and setting off alarm lights? Iles had mentioned to Harpur a while ago a novel and film where people who were terribly injured in a car crash got an extra thrill from undelayed sex in the wrecked vehicle.

Iles would most likely also theorize as Harpur had about the causes of Rose Waverton's impulse – a crisis search for solace – and see it as additional evidence that Waverton had tried to get Manse killed, and might try again. Harpur wondered about that, too, but not with the same certainty and confidence as Iles.

No, spying on couples coupling didn't interest Harpur; or didn't interest him enough to be caught at it and immortalized on film. He supposed that one of them would go back afterwards to find the triumphant freestyle girl. Harpur would try to get behind the Merc once more when they left. He'd have to decide later whether to give an account of things to Iles. The assistant chief didn't know Harpur had started the surveillance. He definitely did not want Iles to find out by having some CCTV footage put in front of him showing Harpur snooping on post-gala intimacy.

EIGHT

Since the death of his wife, Harpur had brought up their two daughters as a single parent, with occasional help from his girlfriend, Denise, a nineteen-year-old undergraduate at the local university. She was cooking breakfast for the four of them this morning. His daughters loved it when Denise stayed overnight. They felt this restored the family to something like what it should be.

Denise didn't live in permanently at Arthur Street, though Harpur and his daughters wished she did. She had a room at Jonson Court, a student accommodation block on campus, and sometimes spent the night there or with friends. In the vacations she'd usually go home to see her mother and father in Stafford for a week or so.

Denise never smoked while preparing meals nor while eating one of them. She ran her life according to some inflexible rules and always insisted that the breakfast bacon should be lean and not more than two fried eggs each. She was only four years older than Harpur's daughter, Hazel, and he suspected Denise didn't greatly like being thought of by the children as a sort of replacement ma. But she never let them see that. She had tact and considerateness. Maybe she remembered from her own fairly recent experience how easily hurt young girls could be. Harpur wondered if she kept the Jonson Court room so as not to become wholly committed to him and Hazel and Jill. That possible reluctance disappointed Harpur, but he understood it, would put up with it. Denise had a life to fashion and she probably didn't plan on confining it to 126 Arthur Street. Today she wore the short blue dressing gown she stored at Harpur's house, thick grey hiking socks and suede desert boots.

Hazel said, 'He has secrets you know, Denise.'

'Well, of course, he has secrets,' Jill said. 'He's police and therefore some matters are private. They got to be.'

'*Have* to be,' Harpur said. He was used to the children

and Denise discussing him almost as if he were not present. Chipping in with some grammar might remind them that he was.

'Yes, have to be,' Jill said.

'But maybe he talks to you, Denise,' Hazel said.

'Of course he talks to Denise,' Jill said. 'Some of it is what's called "pillow talk", that being very one-to-one. But it don't mean he can't still keep some stuff private, because it's how a detective got to be, not blabbing everything relating to cases and that.'

'It *doesn't* mean,' Harpur said.

'Exactly,' Jill said. 'It doesn't mean no secrets, owing to some stuff being to do with the job and what's called "ongoing". Like I said, it got to be.'

'*Has* to be,' Harpur said.

'Yes, *has* to be,' Jill replied. 'That's what I said, Dad. Do you know, Mohammed Ali made fun of how Frazier talked – just to get him mad. Frazier said "gonna" and Ali told him it should be "going to". Then Ali said, "Talk intelligent."'

'Has Dad talked to you, Denise?' Hazel said.

'Regarding what?' Denise said.

'This is to do with the swimming gala,' Hazel said.

'We know one of the kids who was in it. She won all sorts,' Jill said. 'She's in our school. She's all right. She don't get boasty or wanting to be like adored owing to her crawl.'

'*Doesn't*,' Harpur said '*Boastful*'.

'Right,' Jill replied.

'She knows Dad,' Hazel said.

'Well, not knows in the full meaning knows,' Jill said. 'She's seen him on TV news and she recognized him.'

'At the baths,' Hazel said.

'He was watching, but she thinks he wasn't watching the gala, but was watching her mum and dad who were there supporting,' Jill said. 'I don't know how she can be sure of that because her face would be underwater for a lot of the time in the crawl.'

'Between events,' Hazel said.

'No, you haven't spoken about that to me, have you, Colin?' Denise said.

'Olive Waverton,' Hazel replied.

There was a special, large blue teapot the girls brought out when Denise did breakfasts. It had become part of a ritual, like a censer in some church ceremony. The size said 'family' to them. Denise gave refills from it now. Harpur felt there should be priests muttering a litany behind the gentle pouring sound.

'We've asked Dad – kept on at him, but no good,' Hazel said.

'Usually, I don't think we'd ask so strong, not even Hazel, who's a real one for questions to Dad,' Jill said, 'like . . . like what you call it . . .?'

'Interrogation?' Denise said.

'That's it,' Jill said.

'So *strongly*,' Harpur said.

'Yes, strongly,' Jill said, 'like the religious education teacher, real persistent, on who begat who.'

'*Really* persistent,' Harpur said.

'Yes, really,' Jill replied.

'Who begat *whom*,' Harpur said.

'Do they have whoms in the Old Testament?' Jill said. 'Why we kept asking was because this is to do with us, with Hazel and I.'

'Hazel and *me*,' Harpur said.

'No, not you, Dad,' Jill said.

'Just correcting your creaky English,' Hazel said.

'The day after the pool, this kid, Olive, younger than us, comes asking in school – Haze first, then me – asking about Dad – why he's at the gala although his own children – us – are not there, and staring at her mother and father. What this Olive calls "a cop stare, meaning guilty until proved very guilty".'

'I seem to know the name,' Denise said.

'Which?' Hazel asked.

'Waverton,' Denise said.

'How do you mean, *seem* to know,' Hazel said.

Jill said, 'This is what I mentioned. Haze has questions all the time.'

'It's a name I think I've heard around,' Denise replied.

'Around where?' Hazel said.

'See?' Jill said.

'Just around,' Denise said. 'From friends, perhaps.'

'What do you mean, "perhaps"?' Hazel replied.

'This kid, Olive, coming up to us and asking about Dad and we can't answer,' Jill said. 'We didn't even know he was at the gala until this Olive started asking us about it. And she will most likely go to other kids and say he was at the pool and giving a real gaze and we – that's Haze and me—'

'Haze and *I*,' Harpur said.

'Haze and I, Haze and me, whatever, whichever, all of us – that's Haze and I or Haze and me – looking so stupid, not knowing Dad was at the pool at all, and so, it's obvious, not knowing *why* he was there, or why he's eyeballing Mr and Mrs Waverton. This is bad – a kid younger than us knowing stuff about Dad that we didn't.'

'Yes, I think I've heard the name around,' Denise said. She was finishing some black pudding and seemed very thoughtful as she chewed. She was tall – about 5' 9" – with dark hair worn to just above shoulder level, with a small-boned, slight, wiry frame, her face alert and inquisitive, grey-blue eyes, very nicely disposed features. She belonged to a ballet club in the city.

'But Dad hasn't talked to you about the pool?' Jill asked.

'This is the law seeming to apply big attention to Olive's mother and father, so, of course, she's curious and worried,' Hazel said. 'All we can give her is zilch.'

'She said her mum and dad went out before the end of the gala and Dad hurried after them, so we know for sure he must of been interested only in them, not the events,' Jill said.

'Must *have* been,' Harpur said.

'Yes. It's why he's there,' Jill said. 'Maybe they went out to try to get away from his staring. If you go to a gala, you don't want to be stared at all the time by police. Then her mother came back in to collect Olive, but by herself. She thinks that when they drove to the gala there might have been another car on their tail, one person in it, a big man. A Ford Focus. Olive couldn't be sure who it was but does the headquarter's fleet have Focuses, Dad.'

'Why were you tailing them, Dad? That's not the kind of job for a detective chief superintendent, anyway,' Hazel said.

'I told you, there got to be secrets sometimes in copdom. Dad might of wanted to do this tracking on a confidential basis, confidential even from other detectives.'

'Might *have* wanted,' Harpur said

'There's a Bond film called *For Your Eyes Only*,' Jill said.

'So?' Hazel replied.

'It shows that even inside a department, such as, for instance, the detective department, there might be jobs that only one person knows about, which is Dad when he's behind the Wavertons.'

The children left for school. Denise and Harpur washed up and then went back to bed. Denise had nothing at the university until midday and Harpur could fictionalize a few hours doing checks around the borough. Denise lay on the duvet in her clothes and boots for a while, smoking her first cigarette of the day. She said, 'I didn't tell Hazel and Jill but when I hear the name Waverton it's from users at uni, students and staff. He's mid-rank in one of the main firms, isn't he, Col, marshalling pushers? Manse Shale's outfit – the one whose wife and son got shot? Are you hitting the drugs game? But why? I thought Mr Iles wanted a quiet life for the city and, as long as he got it, would ignore the trading. But, then, you're not Mr Iles, are you? Was it about sales of stuff at a children's gala? Does even Mr Iles draw the line at that?'

'This is not the kind of pillow-talk I'm interested in now,' Harpur replied.

'Who needs *any* kind of talk?' she said, taking one final, almighty drag on the cigarette, then standing to stub out the remaining fragment and undressing slowly in a bump n' grind striptease send-up. 'One of the things I love about you, Colin, is that you don't mind if my mouth tastes like an ashtray.'

'What are the other things?'

'Oh, I expect we'll work through the list now, won't we?'

NINE

It was one of those central things about Denise, like the insistence on lean breakfast bacon and the primly enforced limit of two fried eggs, that the love affair with Harpur should be open, undisguised, unfurtive; as she used to say, 'not hole in the corner, and I don't speak as the corner'. So, when someone rang the front door bell, she said, 'I'll go, Col, You need a rest.' She swung out of the bed, put on the blue dressing gown and went barefoot downstairs. Harpur felt delighted with this. She behaved as if she were a normal part of the household and naturally took on routine duties such as answering the door regardless of what she had on or didn't, halfway through the morning. In a while she called out, 'It's a Mrs Waverton, Col.'

'Right,' he said. 'I'll be down in a minute.'

'I'll make some coffee,' Denise said.

Harpur dressed. He took the bit of debris from the cigarette and put it down the lavatory. Then he joined the two of them in the big sitting room. Denise had brought coffees from the kitchen. 'I found your address in the telephone book, Mr Harpur,' Mrs Waverton said.

'Col thinks he should be available,' Denise replied. 'He won't go ex-directory. He claims his nickname is "24/7".'

'It's about the gala,' Rose Waverton said.

'Ah, I've heard something of that,' Denise said. 'Your daughter did very well, I gather.'

'It's not so much about her,' Rose Waverton said.

'If there's something bugging you you're very wise to come here. Colin will do everything he can to help,' Denise said.

Harpur thought she most probably did believe this. She might help Mrs Waverton believe it, or half believe it, too. He felt glad Denise was here and, unless Mrs Waverton objected, he would like Denise to stay, although this would be police business and, as Jill had insisted, some of that should be secret.

'I'm Denise,' she said. 'I know this family very well.'

'I see.'

'And you?'

'Rose.'

The two women, sitting alongside each other on a settee, cup in hand, might have been at a sedate coffee morning somewhere, though Denise was young for that brand of socializing, and not suitably dressed. Rose Waverton, he'd guess, must be at least fifteen years older. Tall – about 5' 9," like Denise – she had mousy-to-blonde hair showing no grey yet. She was blue-eyed, slim, with good, fair skin, her face round, cheerful and friendly when he had seen her at the dancing in the Agincourt; but drawn and troubled now. Women in her sort of marriage often had special troubles. Did they know they were hitching up to a possible villain, but took him just the same? Love is blind? Love is not only blind but stupid? Harpur had never been able to get a proper answer to this. She wore light blue trousers and a crimson top under a white, woollen cardigan.

'Is it presumptuous of me to turn up at your home, Mr Harpur?' Rose Waverton said. 'I didn't dare tell Frank I was coming here.'

'Col expects callers. He's a sort of supplementary Citizens' Advice Bureau.'

'You want to know why I was at the gala,' Harpur replied.

'It . . . puzzled us,' she said. Harpur had an idea she almost said 'frightened us' but de-dramatized it.

'No need,' he said. That would cover both words. 'It's routine only.'

'Routine to attend a kids' swimming gala?' Rose Waverton said.

'I think Col means something of larger scope than that, Rose,' Denise said. She seemed to have grasped at once that Harpur might need her help and Denise instantly began to give it, and to understand what it should be.

'Routine to take a look at one or two people in the various firms,' Harpur said.

'To what purpose?' Rose Waverton asked.

'Under the assistant chief, Mr Iles, we run a unique system here,' Harpur said.

'The businesses, you mean?' she asked.

'Things have to be kept in balance,' Harpur said.

'In balance?' Mrs Waverton said.

'Col will explain, I know,' Denise said.

'There is a non-interference policy, as formulated by Mr Iles,' Harpur said.

'Yes, I think I'd deduced that,' Rose said. It might have been a put-down, but Harpur always ignored put-downs; a technique he'd perfected during conversations with Iles.

'That non-interference is conditional,' Harpur said. 'Mr Iles's policy contains considerable career risk. Not everyone in Her Majesty's Inspectorate of Constabulary or at high governmental level believes that policy acceptable. They watch for, hope for, disaster, enabling them to reverse Mr Iles's initiative, to discredit him, perhaps finish him off.'

'Yes, I think I'd worked that out, too,' Rose said.

'So, it's conditional upon peaceful, normal, restrained behaviour by all concerned,' Harpur replied.

'Yes?' Mrs Waverton said.

'But, obviously, we can't keep an eye continuously on every member of both principal firms,' Harpur said.

'Right,' Mrs Waverton said. She sounded less tense, as if she could see where his explanation was going, and took comfort from it.

'We select one person of significance from either Manse Shale's or Ralph Ember's firm and do a kind of quick check on his or her lifestyle. We assume that the person chosen is reasonably typical of people in both the main outfits. It's our way of assessing the general state of things. Opinion polls work similarly – on a sample. Although our sample is only one, it works. We can assess what the whole business scene here is.'

'You extrapolate from your chosen example,' Denise said. 'Create a larger picture from it.'

'Along those lines,' Harpur replied. 'Denise can give us the professional, learned term. She has a stack of A levels.'

'You mean it was Frank's turn?' Mrs Waverton asked. 'He was a symbol, a touchstone.' She smiled, seemed wholly relieved.

'Temporarily,' Harpur said. 'Why I said "routine". Someone else next time.'

Denise put out a hand and patted Mrs Waverton's arm comfortingly. 'Didn't I tell you Col would explain and calm your anxieties? A family at a swimming gala couldn't be more normal and peaceable, could it? All that innocent water.'

'Thank you, thank you,' Rose Waverton said. She and Denise talked a little about Olive, the swimmer, and then Mrs Waverton stood and put her empty cup on the floor, ready to leave. But, as if suddenly hit by an afterthought, she said, 'Olive told us you followed Frank and me out, Mr Harpur.' She coloured a little.

'Well, yes,' he said.

'Forgive what I'm going to say, but Olive thought I seemed to be hurrying to get away from you,' Rose Waverton said.

'Oh?' Harpur replied.

'But it wasn't that, was it?' Mrs Waverton said.

'Wasn't it?' Harpur said.

'You're very tactful, Mr Harpur. Not something one can always rely on from the police.'

'Ah!' Denise said. She stood, too.

'What?' Harpur said.

'Tactful?' Denise replied.

'So?' Harpur said.

'You wanted a quick shag in the car, Rose. Is that it?' Denise asked earnestly. She would be familiar with that kind of pressing need. Harpur saw he had been brilliantly farsighted to want her in on the conference; she could empathize. 'I don't know why I say "quick". Shags shouldn't be quick, should they? Mussolini thought so, apparently, but look what happened to him: hanged upside down from a lamp post. We're not rabbits. What I mean is you moved very smartly to get a shag in the car – quick in the approach – but then the actual sweet conjoining properly slow until the final stages, naturally, and entirely satisfactory, I'm sure. Col wouldn't peep in. Not his way at all. But, of course, it's a lovely positive part of that profile he needed to build of your hubby at this time. A re-affirmation bonk in a public car park is just the kind of admirable evidence he wanted, isn't it? Wife has an urgent, hot-pussy yen for sex *in* more or less *situ* and hub is there to supply it. A perfect, eloquent moment, "the convergence of the twain", as old Thomas Hardy, the poet, would put it. What kind of car?'

'A Merc.'

'Great! This was a quality experience in two senses,' Denise replied. 'Real leather back seat? So kind to the bare arse.'

'How do you know that?' Harpur asked.

'When you went back in to collect Olive were you looking rather ruffled still, but dewy-eyed and content?' Denise replied. 'Col would have been able to report to Ilesy that he'd witnessed a paradigm vignette, wholly reassuring, even inspiring.'

Mrs Waverton left.

'Homework for me: look up extrapolate, paradigm and vignette,' Harpur told Denise.

'I've got to get dressed and move, Col,' she said. 'Seminar at twelve. That was a gallon of eyewash you gave her, wasn't it? I never thought you'd sink so far into cliché you could say "lifestyle". Frank Waverton's in the frame for something big and very bad, is he? It calls for senior dick Colin Harpur's personal intervention. Poor Rose. I think you're creating a picture of him, yes, but not for the waffle reasons you gave her. Right?'

'A seminar on what?' Harpur replied.

'Lawrence. *Women In Love.*'

'You'll shine.'

TEN

Sitting in a hired Renault Grand Scenic at the civic swimming baths car park, Ralph Ember had done some serious
watching a couple of evenings ago. A banner across the
front of the building had announced a children's gala was
underway now and he'd guessed that Frank and Rose Waverton
had come to cheer on their daughter, Olive. He'd seen a mention
of her in a local paper's list of contestants.

Ralph needed to build an all-round picture of Frank
Waverton. One of the things about Ralph was that he had
scruples. He would never mention these scruples to other
people in a pious, vain way, but Ralph knew he definitely had
considerable scruples, and that these quite often affected his
behaviour. He couldn't carry out his role of the mystery
element who would slaughter Frank without proof that he
deserved it. He didn't consider the reasons given him by Manse
Shale as anywhere near adequate: not much beyond a powerful
hunch. Ralph would admit that Shale's hunches might often
prove right; he'd established a fine, even brilliant firm, and
that would have required intelligent gambling and guesswork
– hunches, in fact. But Ralph demanded something plainer
and more concrete.

That was difficult, obviously. The whole point of the planning
with Manse was that the killer had no motive. Ralph didn't
need a motive, but he did need something to show Waverton
was bad and bad enough to die. That badness might not be
exercised against Ralph but Ralph should be able identify it.
Manse had given him the Waverton family details plus other
backgrounding – the Merc, the hillside jogging, the middling
position in Manse's firm, but Ralph needed a lot extra to this
before he would feel comfy with a mission to kill. Manse's
judgement might have been hit askew by the terrible murder of
his wife and son. In Ralph's view that would be entirely natural.
But it meant that some of Manse's ideas and schemes required

systematic examination and possible reshaping; maybe, even rejection.

Ralph didn't have any armament with him the other night at the baths' parking ground. This had not been a hunting trip; a reconnaissance trip. He wanted to get familiar with Waverton's appearance and with the pattern of his life: his *whole* life, not just business duties and jogging. In this fashion – fragments at a time – he might pick up enough information, enough reliable, specific information, to make Shale's theorizing credible and fit to be acted on. Ralph had remained outside the baths building. He'd felt he would probably get spotted and recognized if he went in. He didn't want Waverton alerted to the fact that he was under surveillance as a potential target.

After about three quarters of an hour he'd seen Frank and his wife come out from the baths and make for their Mercedes. Ralph hadn't started the Renault engine at once, in case the sound drew attention, but he got ready to move out behind them when they left. Perhaps their daughter would be taken home in the school's team vehicle. Ralph's eyes had been focused very closely on Frank and Rose as they walked – seemed to hurry – towards the car, and Ralph didn't notice at first that Detective Chief Superintendent Colin Harpur emerged from the baths behind them but had stopped near the doors.

Ralph had realized Harpur, too, was watching the couple. It amazed and baffled Ember that Harpur should be there. Why would he have an interest in the Wavertons? Was it in any way linked to Shale's theory about Frank, and if so *which* way, for God's sake?

And Ralph's confusion had grown worse still. The Wavertons reached their car and unlocked it then climbed aboard, Rose first, but into the back, not the driving and passenger seats. Into the back! Both! Frank pulled the door shut. Ralph had been too far away to see what might happen inside, but he would deduce. Hell, had the Wavertons got a dogging arrangement with Harpur – that modish, vehicle-based custom where couples, or more than couples, put on a sex performance for others to view? As Ralph understood it, the word referred to 'walking the dog', and stumbling upon people making love. The internet carried plenty of local dogging information. It was clearly a growth industry. Car parks ranked among the favourite venues for these popular, cross-class tableaux. Ralph reckoned that all the sex scandals covered in the media lately showed that unusual sex might affect all sorts. Police could be included, most probably. As a big part of their career, cops were used to spying on people, observing, noting, peeping. Maybe dogging seemed natural to them as an off-duty relaxation.

Did what seemed to be taking place here suggest an arrangement of some sort between Harpur and the Wavertons, a link, an understanding? They'd have to fix a meeting point: 'We'll see you seeing us at the baths car park, Col. We're looking forward to being looked at.' Ralph had tried to work out what such a connection would mean. Harpur and Waverton were buddies? How far did such matiness go? Was it more than to do with Mercedes sex? Ralph felt dazed. He'd come to the baths hoping to get some early glimpses of Waverton's life and style. He would never have expected Harpur to figure at all, let alone in this special, get-an-eyeful role.

Ralph stayed in the Renault and tried to slip a little lower in the driving seat so as not to be obvious. But Harpur hadn't gone audiencing at the Mercedes. He'd watched the Wavertons get into their car and then seemed to have no more to do with it. He walked across the yard to an unmarked Ford saloon and drove away. Bemused more than ever, Ralph continued in his post. After about twenty minutes both doors of the Mercedes opened and the couple got out. They closed the doors. Frank opened the driver's door and climbed in behind the wheel. Rose went into the baths building and in a little while returned with their daughter. She carried a sports bag. The girl got into the passenger seat and Rose went into the back again. Ralph thought she might be enjoying good memories there.

He'd decided they'd go home and he didn't follow but drove to the Monty. The club was crowded. Early release schemes in British jails had been extended to free up room inside and Ralph congratulated and shook hands with three members who had reappeared sooner than expected at the Monty. These were the sort he'd kick out and keep out once he had the club improvement programme in operation. For the present, though, he was their host and hosts had to dish out geniality. A barman had

poured Ralph his usual Kressmann's Armagnac and he took it
to his first-floor office. He'd sat down and thought about the
evening.

It had been obviously wrong to suspect dogging. He considered, instead, that he had witnessed an impressive, unpostponable,
super-tremor act of lovemaking, Rose, perhaps, the initiator;
she had almost sprinted on her way to the Mercedes. Ralph had
wondered how someone with such deep, authentic needs would
be if Frank were wiped out. He didn't have to wonder for long.
She would be desolated. Ralph had found it difficult – more
difficult than ever – to think of killing Frank under the you-
scratch-my-back-I'll-scratch-yours-in-due-course contractual
formula pinched by Manse Shale from the cinema.

ELEVEN

As Harpur had walked towards the unmarked Ford in the swimming bath car park the other evening, he'd noticed Ralph Ember apparently watching the Wavertons. Ralph was in a red Renault Grand Scenic. Harpur hoped he'd given no sign that he'd seen him, but once he was behind the car had taken a glance at the registration number and memorized it. Next day he'd done a check. The car had been hired for a week from a local firm, Easy-Come, Easy-Go in Lavender Street.

For Ralph to avoid using one of his own or his companies' cars suggested he wanted to stay unobserved. For a moment Harpur wondered whether Ralph had some sort of dogging arrangement with the Wavertons, but he'd doubted whether this was Ember's kind of thing. So, what *was* Ralph's kind of thing? Harpur might have understood it all better if it had been Manse Shale in the Renault. No, it was Ember and Ember alone.

Had it been Shale instead, Harpur would have supposed he was witnessing the start of a vengeance exercise; vengeance and a plan to stop any further betrayals. Manse had made his attitude to Frank Waverton very evident at the Agincourt. Why was it, then, Ralph doing the dogging, in its other, gumshoe sense, not Shale; and thorough dogging if he needed the Renault for a week?

Today, Denise was on another overnight and the four of them sat at breakfast again. Harpur said, 'Haze, you had a film on the movie channel a while ago about two men agreeing to do each other's murder.'

'*Strangers On A Train*,' Jill replied.

'Novel by Patricia Highsmith,' Hazel said.

'Film directed by Hitchcock,' Denise said. 'Why are you interested, Col?'

Harpur quartered a fried egg.

'I think it might be another one of those secrets,' Jill said.

'Is it to do with that visit here by Mrs Waverton, Col?'
Denise said.

'Which call here by Mrs Waverton?' Hazel said.

'She looked in the other day,' Denise said.

'Why, Dad?' Hazel said. 'You didn't mention it.'

Harpur busied himself with the egg.

'Yes, another of those secrets,' Jill said.

TWELVE

Ralph Ember returned the hired Renault Grand Scenic to the Easy-Come, Easy-Go premises in Lavender Street. Ralph's wife, Margaret, was to follow in about ten minutes to chauffeur him back to the Monty. Ralph would pay for the hire by credit card but he had a fifty pound note ready, also. The girl doing the paperwork when he originally hired the Renault had been typically shocked and thrilled by his remarkable likeness to the young Charlton Heston.

'I'd have thought you'd want a chariot, not a dull old Renault saloon,' she said. Ralph was used to this type of quip, especially from women. It could be tiresome but he put up with it. She was talking about the film, *Ben Hur*, and Chuck Heston's scenes in a brilliantly fast and dangerous chariot race. It reappeared regularly at Easter on television.

'A chariot?' he'd replied. Almost always Ralph would pretend not to understand such joshing, and would put on a nice, humble show of bafflement. Ralph despised vanity in any form and it would obviously be disgustingly arrogant to act as if he knew he had the magnificent looks of Heston in his prime, although he did know. How could he fail to know when so many people had told him? It could be regarded as perverse to believe himself merely ordinary in appearance. 'Why a chariot?' he said.

'Charlton Heston driving one,' she replied. 'You're his double. I mean before he got elderly and mouthing off about the right to own a gun.'

'I've definitely heard of him,' Ember had said.

'And *El Cid*,' she replied.

'He's in that one?'

'Near the end, he's dead but, just before a battle, they strap him to his favourite horse. His troops will observe him, seeming as warlike and strong as ever, and their morale will stay upbeat. He looked great even when a corpse.'

'That's true flair,' Ralph replied. 'Not many have it.'

'I'm sure you'd have it,' she'd replied.

'You're very kind. The horse would have been damn puzzled to get a deado on his back, no thigh pressure or rein-tug. The animal must have known all the battle moves now El Cid no longer directed; like an armoured car driven by a tailor's dummy.'

She was about twenty-three or -four, almost pretty and with a tidy arse. Ralph had thought he might keep her in mind. She wore a wedding and engagement ring but he considered these would probably be regarded by her as not too restrictive when she had a chance of attention from a beautifully replicad Heston. Ralph could imagine her calling out triumphantly to friends at some charity function, 'I fucked Chuck!'

She'd plainly been very intrigued by the long scar on one side of Ralph's face, from his cheek up to his temple. Like many women, she'd clearly wanted to finger this and had raised the rings hand towards it but then drew back, perhaps afraid she would seem disrespectful – a hire firm clerk confronted by Charlton Mark 2. Ralph could have told her that many women had, in fact, run their hands over the old wound, as if they hoped to find a combination code that might open it up and let them get inside him. This was something else Ralph tolerated extremely well. He would never condemn such reverential contact as a grope.

For now, anyway, he wanted her cooperation in a different fashion. He felt glad he'd made this early, very useful personal contact with her. As she prepared the car hire bill and they were alone in her office Ralph said, 'It would interest me greatly to know whether anyone had asked for the identity of the hirer. Probably you get that kind of inquiry sometimes.'

'Well, yes we do.'

'And?'

'Obviously, we can't disclose such information.'

'Except when it's the police, I expect.'

'Well, yes, the police would be different.'

She was seated at a computer to prepare the account and Ralph bent forward a little so that if she wanted to she could fondle and/or stroke his scar, and at the same time he put the fifty pound note on the side of the table. 'Could you suggest a name,' she said, 'so I wouldn't actually be telling you, only confirming.'

Ralph knew this was a regular trick in business when someone wanted to leak something confidential without actually leaking it. 'Harpur,' he replied.

She didn't speak or nod but blinked unambiguously. She picked up the fifty so as to make space for the card machine and passed Ralph the bill. He keyed in his payment. She receipted the account, and raised her right hand this time and very briefly touched up the old wound. 'Poor Chuck,' she said, 'yet I'm sure an honourable, even noble injury.' Ralph couldn't work out where the fifty had gone but it was no longer in sight.

'I'll know where to come when I want a hiring next,' Ralph said.

'Oh, yes, do, but surely you have a car, cars, of your own.'

'Here's one of them now,' Ralph replied. Margaret in the Lexus drew up outside.

'So why?' she asked. 'Is it something exciting? I mean, the police involved.'

'Not a Charlton Heston scale drama, I'm afraid. Routine,' he said.

'Routine, how? I don't understand.'

No, he couldn't expect her to understand, assumed she wouldn't understand, and definitely wouldn't understand from *him*, although it centred on the Renault. At the swimming bath car park, Ralph had seen Harpur walk towards his own vehicle after watching the Wavertons enter the Merc. He behaved as though he hadn't seen Ralph but Ralph knew he had undoubtedly seen and recognized him well enough; and, when he'd got around the back Harpur did a sharp, remember-it gaze at the registration, he, visible in the rear-view mirror, doing it.

'Is that your wife?' the Easy-Come, Easy-Go girl asked. 'I expect she gets a lot of trouble with other women making approaches, wanting to be . . . well, to be associated in an intimate manner with a sort of star.'

'I don't think she regards me as a star, not of any sort.'

THIRTEEN

While waiting, waiting, waiting for Ralph Ember to act, Shale had kept an occasional watch on Waverton, mainly in case the sod gave any sign that he was helping line up another attempt on Manse – one that really got to him this time. Shale needed to be ready. He carried a Heckler and Koch 9 mm Parabellum pistol most days and nights now. And he had two of his heavies in the firm on continuous armed stand-by.

He'd noticed the Waverton name in a newspaper list of competitors at a school swimming bath gala and had guessed the parents of the child might turn up in support. Lying low in the car park there he had watched the Wavertons come out from the building and get into the back of their S-class Mercedes for what seemed to Manse a bit of uncontrollable, married bliss nooky. He'd heard that Mercedes cars did turn some people on. Manse thought it must be to do with the bonnet symbol which looked like a pair of open legs, with a third stiff vertical line spare, so far; a saucy hint to horny couples to get things completed on the rear seat. Manse had wondered sometimes whether sex counsellors dealing with what was termed dysfunction should advise people to get a Mercedes, not necessarily new and therefore pricey, but of any age because the badge would be on all models.

Harpur had emerged from the baths very soon after the Wavertons. He'd stared towards them until they disappeared into the Merc, then walked to his own, or the job's, unmarked Ford saloon. Back home in the old rectory Manse had a record of all unmarked police cars and, as far he could remember, there were several Fords, saloons and estates, so this could certainly be one of them. Harpur had seemed to loiter behind a Renault Grand Scenic, perhaps putting the reg into his memory. Police were trained to have good memories; also how to adjust what they remembered when a case needed that. The car park seemed to contain a lot of tasty people tonight.

Manse had not given much notice to the Renault previously. The police didn't use Grand Scenics, and he could be sure he'd have no record of this one in that file. He also kept notes on cars used by all personnel in his own and Ralph Ember's firms and there might be mention of a Grand Scenic, or Scenics, in one of those lists, but he couldn't say definitely. Manse knew that some youngsters would view him as pitifully behind the times in relying on handwritten notes. If he'd gone fully electronic he would be carrying all these records around with him in a chip and there'd be no need to try to recall elementary facts like this. He'd get them instantly on the screen of his phone.

But Manse liked paper and pen or pencil. Reading and writing had come quite late to Shale. He'd been on an adult literacy course in his late twenties and the pleasure enjoyed from earning an approved standard in both, backed by diplomas, continued its grip on him. The woman running the course, not young, was especially helpful and friendly, without ever trying to get his pants off. He loved jotting down information in a loose-leaf book and loved, too, reading stories, hardback and paperback, such as the tales about a boy brought up by wolves; and another book to do with savage kids marooned on a desert island after a plane crash. He didn't care if these volumes had no pictures. It was the words he thrilled to, the ways they followed each other very nicely in a little procession, linking up, helping the next along towards a full stop or exclamation mark. There wouldn't be no stories if they didn't. Words was great even on their own, but they needed to join up in a line if they was going to tell you something. Now and then people would come up to you and say, 'Could I have a word?' They didn't really mean that, though, as if they was asking you for a word, a single word. In fact, they wanted to *give* not take and what they wanted to give was not just a word but a string of words which could add up to what might be worth listening to. Paragraphs delighted him – their bulkiness and the way they'd sometimes finish off with only a couple of words where they got to their end showing the paragraph had said all it wanted to say.

One of Manse's big regrets was that he'd never felt confident enough to read to the children when they was small. It wouldn't of been good for them to hear their dad spluttering and blundering over a page. Children had to be able to admire their dad not regard him as a joke. By the time he'd reached a fair standard Laurent and Matilda could read better than he could, so he'd become surplus. Although he had recommended the Mowgli stuff to them he didn't believe they'd ever tried it, and it was too late for Laurent now, of course. Manse still had trouble with the spoken language occasionally or oftener, but he was gradually sprucing that up. If he caught himself saying, for instance, 'I done it,' he would repeat at least ten times at mutter strength, 'I did it.' Although most might understand what he meant even when he said 'I done it,' that sort of mistake could put a mark on you, like not wiping snot off of the end of your nose. People noticed and made remarks to others about you. Manse Shale's mother used to worry a lot about people making remarks. She seemed to mean the remarks could only be bad.

Harpur's bit of a loiter at the back of the Scenic had given Manse a message. It said that Harpur didn't know this car but he *did* know who was in it and was interested in who was in it. Who was in it, Manse had discovered, looked like Ralph Ember, and for a couple of moments then Manse had wondered whether this car park was Ralph's chosen killing ground and at last he meant to do Waverton. Manse had soon come to correct this notion, though.

He guessed that Harpur would have expected a different vehicle for Ralph. Like Manse, the police would know Ralph's usual cars: a Subaru, a Lexus, a couple of VW Golfs; these two were German but didn't have the same power to sex people up as with the German Merc because a VW lacked that badge. VW meant people's car, but people in general as drivers, not people fuck-driven.

Manse had thought the Scenic must be either brand new or hired. But then he'd realized that the reg made it a year old at least. Hired, then. Harpur would want to know why Ralph had a rented car. To get anonymity? Manse, also, would also like to know why a rented car. To get anonymity? Why anonymity? The answer to that seemed plain: Ralph was watching the Wavertons and didn't want them to know he was. Harpur would probably reach the same answer.

But that answer really angered Shale then and now for two

reasons. There might be more. (a) Manse reckoned Ralph had come not immediately to do the kill but to have a serious lurk, a lurk he hoped would stay secret, owing to the Grand Scenic. He'd set himself up there to spy because he would not accept an absolute statement from Manse that Waverton was the traitor they had to track down and wipe out. No, not track down. This Manse had already done. It was the whole fucking point. Manse had carried out the discovery of the filthy facts and all Ralph had to do was kill, not dawdle about there in a Renault like deep, confidential surveillance.

In Manse Shale's opinion, no surveillance at all by Ralphy Ember had been needed. Surveillance flung an insult to Manse because it said more or less straight out in a sort of hurtful blurt that his assessment of the Waverton situation might be bollocks and had to be checked, maybe even chucked. Ralph had decided to get his own picture of Frank Waverton by putting him under special watch. No wonder he picked a Grand Scenic. He wanted a grand scene for Waverton, a grand scene created by Ralph, the big-headed sod. All Ralph's energy and purpose had to go to this game-playing and most likely he would never actually *do* anything, such as the central, prime matter of slaughtering Frank Waverton on a neat and comfortable exchange basis. He could act like he was most probably *going* to see to Waverton, but not quite yet, possibly not ever, because he didn't have the degree of info that could convince his mighty, panicking brain.

There was a phrase used in boxing: 'he left it all on the gymnasium floor', meaning a defeated fighter had put all his energies into preparation for the scrap, but was spent and useless when it came to the actual bout. Like Ralphy?

(b) Harpur. Manse had tried to guess why the cop was there. It could not be a dogging arrangement with the Wavertons, no matter how fashionable dogging had become among all classes, as people grew bored by TV and DVDs. Harpur had stayed a long way from the Mercedes, although he knew Frank and Rose were in there probably satisfying each other without what was known as stint. This might be another popular element in Merc sex, it was stintless.

Perhaps Harpur and Iles still wanted to find who had ordered the Jag ambush in Sandicott Terrace – the messed-up ambush that killed Naomi and Laurent. Although shadowing people like the Wavertons was not the kind of basic duty a Detective Chief Super would normally do, Harpur might be acting on an instinct, not proper evidence, and he'd find it tough to explain to his officers why he wanted Waverton tailed.

Or Manse had thought it might be an Iles instinct. People said Iles was very strong on sensing things – things not always visible to others. Iles had nearly got himself killed right after the Sandicott incident, trying to arrest the gunman[3], and he was the sort who'd keep searching for the master thug behind the hitman. Iles didn't mind being regarded as laidback – a phrase Manse had heard recently – but Iles wouldn't fancy being laid out. Possibly, he and Harpur had come to believe Frank was the one who could give a lead. Iles might have told Harpur to do some digging. The difference between them two and Manse was that he didn't just *believe* Waverton might be the disgusting, disloyal link. Manse felt certain of it, and felt fearful of it

That's why it had so gravely pissed him off to see Ralphy there, once it had become plain that he was not in position to do Waverton. Ralph's presence brought risk – stupid, unnecessary risk. That risk had become very obvious when Harpur had identified Ralph in the Grand Scenic and got the number plate into his memory so he could do a trace and confirm who'd done the hiring. Because of Ember's mad and brazen decision to come to the car park, the police would see a connection between him and Frank Waverton; just what the Manse–Ralph deal aimed to conceal; in fact, to make impossible. All fucking ego, that was Ralph. He'd be determined to handle matters his way, but his way could be clumsy and jinxed.

Education. Ralph had some, and he used to let Manse know he had some. This didn't mean the kind of reading and writing classes Manse went to. Higher. Manse believed the word for it might be 'tertiary', meaning top level. Ralph had even joined the university down the road on what was called a mature students' degree scheme. Ralph had given it up for a while because he needed to do hands-on at his businesses. Sales had really took off lately, especially charlie. Manse's own companies had seen the

[3] See *I Am Gold*

same lovely surge. He had read somewhere not long ago that human beings breathed through only one nostril at a time and the body switched automatically between the two. Manse had considered this very good news because it meant one nostril at least was always free, ready to welcome a quality snort.

Although for now Ralph had jacked in uni, as he called it – like he was a student kid – he still talked about the lectures, and profs and books he'd read. He said the uni had begun to teach him how to think in a better way than before. And any bugger could spot the results of this in the matter of Waverton. Ralph had to mull, weigh up, dither, delay, assess, postpone; *think* a lot in that new educated, but-on-the-other-fucking-hand style, and *do* nothing.

It worried Shale that perhaps his daughter, Matilda, would think he was feeble not to have completed a revenge response on them who had caused the murder of her step-mother and brother. She'd probably get some mockery about it at school. Although she had never reproached Manse for the apparent failure, he feared that's what she would think. Matty might consider him weak, yellow, contemptible. Children could be polite and very considerate about what they said and what they didn't, but they also saw situations very simply and starkly.

That turn-and-turn-about project with Ralph had been designed to achieve necessary retaliation in the safest style possible: Waverton would get his head blown off but not by anyone blatantly motivated. However, Ralph seemed set on ignoring the pleasant, undemanding little execution scheme. Shale thought he might have to go for an alternative.

He'd seen Rose Waverton leave the Merc and go into the baths building, her clothes in entirely decent order and no sign of knee trembling. Frank climbed out of the rear and took his place behind the wheel. Rose had come back with their daughter carrying her gear in a sports bag. Interestingly, Rose chose to get into the back of the Merc, perhaps to try re-living solo the last half hour or so there. The car moved away. After a minute the Renault left, too.

FOURTEEN

Shale would often do his best to imagine how Matty saw things these days. There was just the two of them in the old rectory now as long as that meandering cow, Sybil, didn't try to come back; which she had attempted a short while ago when her love life was in a dud gap between some roofer or surgeon or snooker champion and some crooner or judge or hairdresser or Third World ambassador. A sly crawl back by Syb was something else Manse had to be ready for, and ready to kill.

Trauma – that must be the word for what battered Matilda during and after Sandicott Terrace. Trauma meant injuries, but especially to the mind. Shale knew he had to be very understanding and full of support where Matty was concerned. This young girl had caught a lot of blood and fragments when Naomi and Laurent got shot. Most likely she would want to hear of other blood and fragments from the foul creep who'd caused the Sandicott Terrace blood and fragments.

Manse fretted that his daughter might be in, say, a religious education lesson at school about the happy miracles in the Bible such as turning the water into wine, but all the same she'd be thinking of ripping some bastard apart with automatic fire. Shale realized that what he, on his own, absolutely on his own, had to care for with proper tenderness and tact was a mind that must have been assaulted terribly that day and not just by the blood and fragments. Although Manse would admit he wasn't no qualified psychiatrist he saw that the way to make sure the trauma for Matty didn't continue must be to reach what was referred to as 'closure'. And most probably closure could only come with the destruction of the link man, Waverton.

Of course, the main objective was to get whoever the linkman had been linked to. The chief. Manse reckoned that, if Waverton could be finished off, the people he'd been disgustingly informing to would have to find some other way of attacking

Manse and his firm, their objective to grab it, naturally. Drugs were what was known as a growth industry and companies like Manse's looked very desirable to greed-merchants. They believed in growth – of their loot. Manse thought that, without Waverton, the original invaders would make an even bigger mess-up of the campaign. And, now that Manse and his people were expecting the evil work, they could intercept it and, maybe, find where the plan and the orders came from.

The removal of Waverton was an important first move. It should lead to those bigger, cleansing events. Also, because Waverton was local, Matilda and her chums would be able to see that an effective revenge operation had been carried out on their, so to speak, doorstep. They would be entitled to regard that as closure. Matilda's mind would benefit, for sure. She would no longer have to think of him as a useless, dishonourable twirp. But so much for the immediate present depended on thoughtful, paralysed Ralph.

FIFTEEN

This dread of being downgraded, even despised, by his daughter for failing to avenge Naomi and Laurent had become obsessive with Shale. Because she and he were the only ones left at the rectory his longing for her respect mounted, and for the approval needed to keep it. Children could be very harsh and unforgiving. He knew. He remembered this from when a child himself. One terrible notion dominated his thinking now. Did Matilda assume he felt secretly thankful to the gunman for blasting his wife and son instead of him; and assume also that having been spared once he would avoid further risk and play along meekly with things as they were? That line of pathetic reasoning would sicken Matilda. It sickened Shale. He'd never felt like that about Naomi and Laurent's death, had he? For God's sake, no, no, no.

Agonizing like this, he grew more and more convinced that Ralph would never act. The deaths-swap scheme might have to be dropped. Time, success, education had made the bugger soft, Shale decided. If Waverton was to be wiped out – and he *was* to be – Shale would possibly have to do it himself. To hell with go-nowhere parking lot observation sessions.

Word went to chosen people in the business about an all-night rave planned for the Binnacle, an abandoned hotel on the foreshore. Confidentiality was crucial or the police would seal off the site and stop the party before it started. But, obviously a rave needed good stuff as well as the so-called music, and Shale's company had received the whisper.

Manse thought he could spot a chance here. He didn't mean just a routine chance to trade, but a bigger issue, the biggest, in fact. Leadership. In Manse's opinion this ability to see and grab a sudden opportunity was the main quality of true leadership. He'd come across the word 'gravamen' lately, indicating the very heart of a situation. Well, as gravamens went, this skill at glimpsing and using fresh ways forward was probably the most precious gravamen for a chief.

Of course, Manse would admit that now and then this type of gravamen could lead a supremo into disaster. 'Fuhrer' was the German term for leader and, obviously, Hitler's gravamen turned out catastrophic, when he decided the time could not be more right for an attack on Russia during World War Two. All the same, usually that gravamen operated well; often very, very well. He would send a dealer unit to the Binnacle, yes, and he'd put Waverton in charge.

It wasn't the kind of crude scrum Manse normally attended personally but he thought this one might offer fine conditions for doing Waverton and getting clear. There'd be hundreds of kids present, in the building and spilling out into the hotel grounds, most of them dazed by the din and dosage, too intent on the merrymaking to notice very much of what went on around them. He would make a concealed approach; get into some dark clothes. He could drive to a spot a short way down the coast and walk back on the beach towards the hotel, then wait out of sight.

Waverton might emerge from the shindig to take a piss; obviously, the Binnacle's toilets wouldn't be working. Or he could have copped-on with some crack-happy, shag-happy girl customer and led her away for some privacy. Admittedly, that might make things a little more difficult for Shale. A double-handed shooting accuracy stance would be needed. He'd take a 9mm automatic. He was reasonably efficient with this model and used it regularly for target practice. It worried him that a girl might suddenly find herself blood-soaked and snuggled up to a deado. He hoped he could get Waverton alone, but he wouldn't let consideration for the girl spoil what might be a perfect, delayed moment otherwise.

At home in the rectory, Manse hummed to himself an old song, 'Oh, I do like to be beside the seaside.'

SIXTEEN

Ralph Ember heard about an up-coming rave the next day, or rather night, at the one-time chic coastal hotel and restaurant, the Binnacle, closed and empty for a long while now and well on its way to dereliction. Ralph always received a tip-off when this kind of event was planned, so he could send some pushers with a range of quality gear. Manse Shale's firm got an invitation, too. It wasn't the type of party Ember would usually manage on the spot himself, but he did think he might take a discreet look on this one-off occasion.

He decided he'd shoulder-holster his 8-round Walther pistol for the trip. It was a gun with no history, except for the original purchase. It had never been used other than in target practice. He'd thought his gun-carrying days had gone. He kept the Walther as a safeguard only. He liked its feeling of balance and solidity, and hadn't bothered with any of the pistols offered by Shale. There were weapons by Smith and Wesson and Heckler and Koch that he admired almost as much, but lately he had gone for the Walther. Naturally, he'd get rid of it immediately afterwards if he killed with the Walther at the rave. Getting rid of a pistol was not all that easy, but a couple of headlands always had a good water depth even at low tide, and the Walther might end up on the sea bottom there. Possibly he'd give an S. and W. or an H. and K. a turn as replacement. Although Ralph had a definite fondness for Walthers he didn't award them exclusive status and behave as if he had to have a Walther or nothing. Ralph would regard that as absurd.

He found the hotel on his ordnance survey map and saw it could be approached from the rear over a couple of fields. It would be dark, but he'd take a torch as well as the Walther and an approach shouldn't be difficult. He'd leave his car a fair distance from the Binnacle and walk, then lie low somewhere and watch. The rave organizers would have brought a lighting system, and Ralph thought he might get some luck and spot

Waverton clear of the crowd. He would need a piss, or he might have picked up a girl.

Ember felt confused at the way his attitude to the Waverton assassination programme had swung about recently. He could present himself with a list of the arguments against the 'strangers' plan, and they might for a while convince him that the scheme was mad and should be put to sleep. He'd remind himself that Manse Shale's supposed evidence against Waverton amounted to hardly anything. And Ralph thought of the terrible impact Waverton's death would have on Rose, his wife, and their child, Olive. Wasn't Ralph himself a family man? If women hadn't been so excited and pushy because of his looks, Ralph reckoned he would have been totally faithful to Margaret. He didn't think she would accept his arguments that episodes with other women were really only a kind of politeness towards them, a sort of kindly duty, an obligation. Always he came back to the family.

Although he could rehearse these exceptionally logical and humane objections to the slay plan, ultimately Ralph found he had to ignore them. He still felt nudged, and more than nudged, towards a part in Shale's cleansing scheme. There was one extremely crux point about Ralph Ember: nothing could motivate him more powerfully than the need to prove – to himself, and perhaps to others – that those filthy fucking nicknames, Panicking Ralph and – above all – Panicking Ralphy were undeserved and slanderously evil. Continually he looked for ways to nullify those outrageous smears.[4] To have agreed to Manse Shale's proposal and then to wriggle out looked, didn't it . . . looked like panic? He could think of the withdrawal as logical and humane, but that's not how Manse would see it, nor the people he told. 'Typical Ralphy,' they'd think and say. 'Ralph Ember to a T.' 'Yellow.' 'Craven.' 'All blowsy talk.' 'Scaredy cat.' 'Chicken.'

He would not bring all that shit upon himself. He meant to escape from the slur and lies. He must grab this chance. To have spotted it was the result of genuine, even unique, leadership flair. Now, he must go that next distance and produce action

[4] See *Disclosures*

from this flair. What seemed to Ralph very feasible was a well-concealed spot at the Binnacle tomorrow night, a sighting of Waverton, preferably alone, but not necessarily, and the sudden, thought-free, irresistible impulse to pull out the Walther and give him three or four bullets in the chest and head. If he was with a girl, Ralph would try everything to avoid hurting her but he wouldn't – mustn't – let that prevent the required strike on Waverton. Some might maintain that any girl who went with the traitor Waverton should not expect a guarantee of safety, anyway. If she were injured or killed it could be regarded as collateral damage. Ralph would not take that line himself: too savage. But he would have a priority and nothing should interfere with it. Sod logic. Sod humaneness. As he helped out at the Monty bar he hummed an old popular song, 'It's a lovely day tomorrow.'

SEVENTEEN

Manse Shale, crouched behind rocks on the beach in front of the Binnacle, heard and saw a string of police cars, sirens blaring, blue lights flashing, arrive in a rush at the hotel's main entrance and a dozen officers pile out, some uniformed, some not, and dash into the building. A fire engine appeared soon after and ambulances.

Christ, Shale thought, has Ralphy actually done him at last? This had become no place to be. Manse got clear and started the hurried walk back to his car.

EIGHTEEN

Ralph Ember, under a hedge at the side of the Binnacle heard and saw a string of police cars, sirens blaring, blue lights flashing, drive fast to the hotel's main entrance. About a dozen uniformed and plain-clothes officers rushed into the hotel. A fire engine also appeared and ambulances.

My God, Ralph thought, has Manse lost patience and shot Waverton? This was not a good place to be. Ralph got clear and began the walk back quickly over the fields to his car.

sidling away somewhere, equals provocation of a murder. But she certainly was lovely enough to cause a jealousy killing by knife or napalm. He switched off the light. 'Iles would probably regard where we now are as one of those mean streets, rather than a totally confidential one,' he said.

'I think I must go down on you in it then,' she said.

'So, you're a private dick?'

'I hope *you* are, Col.'

TWENTY-ONE

Iles said, 'The fuckers will try to get me for this, Col.'

'Which fuckers did you have in mind, sir?'

'The entirety. All of them. They'll come after me in a slavering, howling pack.'

'I'd bet you can see them off.'

'Who?'

'Those you meant, sir. The slaverers.'

'Her Majesty's Inspectorate of Constabulary, the Home Office, the *Daily Mail*. I'm suddenly an obvious target.'

'Get you for what, sir?'

'This death.'

'The boy at the Binnacle?'

'Of course, the boy at the Binnacle.'

'But you weren't even present, were you? I heard you'd given up going to raves and that you get your kicks elsewhere now.'

'Try to understand what occurred there, would you, please?'

'A three-blow killing.'

'"Three-blow". How admirably accurate! How numerate. How forensic.'

'Thank you, sir.'

'That's how people at your rank think, isn't it, Harpur? You call it "the nitty-gritty".'

'I went to evening classes in nitty-grittyness.'

'All credit to you for getting the count exactly right – not one, not seven, not twenty-four. Three.'

'Thank you, sir.'

'But I'm afraid I have to think more broadly, more deeply, Col. Polity – how society works, its pluses, its minuses. I have to focus on polity.'

'I've heard people murmur in awe after meeting you for the first time, sir. "That Mr Iles, such breadth of vision, such depth of insight, such attention to polity. He and polity were made for each other."'

'The circs, Col?' Iles replied.

'An all-night party. Or would-be all-night. An incident made that impossible.'

'Yes, I think the stabbing can reasonably be referred to as an incident. It has the qualities of an incident, namely, something happened.'

'Incidents are like that,' Harpur said.

'Like what?'

'Something happens.'

'There's a novel called *Something Happened*, Harpur.'

'That's just the author boasting. Something *ought* to happen in novels or they're not novels, they're pamphlets run to seed.'

'Now you're in this analytical mood, I wonder if we can take a lesson from the hotel name, Binnacle,' Iles replied. 'What does a binnacle mean to you, Harpur?'

'Aboard ship, show me a compass and I'll show you binnacles.'

'Yes, binnacles house the compass. And what does a compass have to do with?'

'Direction, guidance,' Harpur said. 'It tells the captain of a ship to turn left at Africa.'

'And this imagined, binnacled compass; in which direction would it take us, to where does it guide us, as regards the Binnacle Hotel?'

'To the rave scene and some indiscreet behaviour, followed by rage and violence.'

'That's what I mean, Col, when I say they'll try to get me for this.'

'Which?' Harpur replied.

'Which what?'

'Which will they try to get you for – the indiscreet behaviour, the rage, the violence?'

'That indiscretion, that rage, that violence – what caused them, Col?'

'Some people were brain-dead on Ecstasy, weed or coke, or a mix, possibly, even, H.'

'Exactly, Col.'

'Thank you, sir.'

'I run a domain where Ralph and Manse are famously allowed

to market their recreational products without interference or hindrance. In exchange I demand tranquillity and order: if possible, no blood on the pavement or the floor of an abandoned hotel. Yes, if possible.'

'A friend of mine was talking about order only the other day. Fortinbras. That's *Young* Fortinbras, obviously, not his dad. It's one word, Fortinbras. Not fought in brass, like an early, very weighty flak jacket.'

'Which friend?'

'Oh, yes, a knowledgeable friend on matters such as the Fortinbrases and Marlowe.'

'A friend of which gender?'

'We can all learn from friends,' Harpur replied.

'Your student *inamorata*, Denise Prior, aged nineteen and evidently with a taste for vastly older men? She's on Garland's list of Binnacle witnesses. You don't mind her going to unbridled sessions of that Binnacle sort without you?'

'*Old* Fortinbras was dead,' Harpur replied, 'and unable to help bring back some order in Denmark.'

'What order was present at the Binnacle, what tranquillity?'

'Those qualities took a beating, no question, sir.'

'My enemies will chortle uncontrollably.'

'Uncontrollably chortle at the savage death of a kid of twenty? What kind of people *are* they?'

'Who?'

'Your enemies.'

'The death of the kid of twenty they will cite as blatant evidence that my – our – tolerance regime failed. At the Binnacle we had units from both the most distinguished local firms peaceably selling their gear in a well-established, convivial way; a delightful example of our happy, positive practice. Perhaps Ralphy and Shale were there themselves to supervise.'

'We haven't anything to suggest that.'

'But suddenly this fine tradition becomes of no relevance, doesn't it? What I'm saying, Harpur, is that despite these splendid, settled conditions, a completely unpredictable, virtually random event at a drugs-related hooley can make it look as if I've – we've – failed in my – our – attempt to maintain public safety through a bargain with the snort traders.

'The knifing has nothing to do with commercial rivalry. It's not an aspect of turf war between the companies. They have grown out of such primitive, wasteful battling. No, we're dealing with a sex sequence. Simply that. And this sex sequence and its murderous result are probably – no, definitely, yes, definitely – fuelled by my – our – permissive drugs formula.

'Now, do you see why I envisage that triumphalist, malevolent chortling? This is chaos theory, Harpur – a seemingly minor event, such as a love squabble among youths, leads to catastrophe of major, appalling dimensions.'

'Chaos theory: that's the one about a moth landing slightly too hard on a basket of laundry in an Amazonian rainforest, causing a chain effect that eventually melts an igloo in Iceland, isn't it? Moths are a bugger. However, things might not turn out as badly as you think, sir,' Harpur replied.

'It's worse than I've described, Col. Garland says that talk during a pause in the aggro was about Shale's guy, Frank Waverton, possibly having provided the road map and route for the slaughter in error of Naomi Shale and the child, Laurent. Waverton is the one who might be able to tell us who set all that up. It's my priority, Col. And he was there, at the Binnacle, attempting to bring calm, but ultimately ignored because of his bad history; bad *possible* history. We have one disaster linked to another and all of it taking place on my – our – ground, Harpur.

'When I mention "polity", this is what I m getting at, Col. I will be hunted, hounded, stalked. Critics will observe and will announce at max volume that my – our – patch is in decline and about to fall. They'll pronounce that there is something rotten in the bailiwick of Desmond Iles, and they'll call for a Young Fortinbras figure to take over and put things right – some jumped-up jerk from the Met, most likely.'

Iles wanted to sit in on the interview/interrogation of the twenty-year-old arrested at the Binnacle. Harpur and the ACC were in a Toyota, Iles driving, on their way to Fonton police station at the northern edge of their ground. To avoid a media siege, it was normal practice to use an undisclosed, outlying, suburban nick for this kind of major inquiry, rather than the headquarters building in the city centre.

Iles had on a silver-buttoned, thin-lapelled, double-breasted, navy blazer, grey slacks, a country-pursuits yellow, tan and dark-red check shirt and large-knot, grey-black woollen tie. It was an outfit that would impress many, Harpur thought, not just a kid being questioned about a fatal knifing.

But Harpur also thought that even if Iles hadn't spoken as he did just now, his fine ensemble couldn't conceal a bad tumble in his morale and Desilesian, bombastic arrogance. Although his custom-made blazer enfolded him lovingly, the cosy slope of its shoulders impeccably right, Harpur could detect a bit of a slump in the way he sat at the wheel. The blazer did its expensive best to present him as elegantly formidable and intemperate, but today its best was not quite good enough.

Occasionally, the assistant chief's Napoleonic confidence and Hitlerite vanity would desert him like this. The reversal always frightened Harpur. The city needed Iles's profound cockiness and his hinted inclination to hit the shit out of anyone who irritated him, particularly local government officers and vicars. The ACC seemed especially forceful with the gear stick this morning, as if to prove he still had all his powers undimmed, boisterous. Harpur wasn't fooled, though. He regarded this sort of near breakdown as similar to those moments when the ACC fell into convulsive despair at the cruelty to Madame Butterfly. Iles could strut, Iles could falter. There were times when Harpur discerned unmistakeable signs of humanity in the assistant chief. It was not something Harpur would tell him because almost inevitably he would translate 'signs of humanity' as signs of weakness, signs of faltering.

He said, 'You'll remember that line from *The Godfather*, Col.'

'Many a line in that film, sir. That's the thing about films – the actors need lines.'

'"Keep your friends close but your enemies closer",' Iles replied. 'I'm thinking of Shale's enemies here, not my own, though God knows there are enough of them. Some unsubtle people might find it impossible to understand why Manse retains Waverton in his firm if he suspects dear Frank helped prepare the Sandicott ambush. Reason? "Suspects" is not the same as knowing. Manse has some principles. Perhaps he wouldn't act without solid evidence.

'Also, there's *The Godfather* advice. If Waverton is still in the firm Manse can watch him and spot whether he's working to create another attack, correcting that first cock-up – now, Manse RIP. Plus, Shale will be constantly aware of where Waverton is, in case one day Manse does want him killed. He'll be wherever he is then because Manse has put him there. So convenient.

'It could be, couldn't it, Col, that Manse sent him to the Binnacle because the stoned, swirling, splintering crowd and the din might make it an ideal background for slaughter? Maybe, unfortunately for Manse, another, unforeseeable slaughter changed the nature of things and made destruction of Waverton at that juncture too difficult. He'll have been looking for obscurity among the crowd, but all at once there'd be no obscurity, a swarm of cops and paramedics.

'What I have to consider constantly, Harpur, is that enemies – mine this time – see us as incapable of getting the boss-man or woman behind the two Sandicott murders, and seemingly content that we finished off the nobody who actually did the shoot: a fall-guy. We look smug, Col, we look slack and torpid, ready to settle for too little in exchange for a quiet life. We might even look corrupt – paid by someone not to push inquiries too hard and too high. And then, to magnify their case against me – us – we get this shambolic fight and knifing at a drug-drenched do which I – we – helped set up by letting Manse and, or Ralph Ember stock it with their produce. That could be spun by enemies as not just blind-eyeing but assisting.'

They had reached the Fonton district on the border of their realm.

Harpur said, 'But you told me all sorts of important voices support your line on drugs, sir.'

'On *faute de mieux* legalizing? Of course they do, Col. The heavyweight magazine, the *Economist,* the Advisory Council On Drugs, some top doctors and health profs. But they are not the law. The law says something different. The law forbids. *We* are the law, Harpur. It's in our hands.'

'Someone historic said these should be "*good* hands".'

'George Savile, Marquis of Halifax, seventeenth century. I didn't know you did deep reading, Col. Denise has been giving you seminars, has she, as well as the standard comforts? What does the word mean, Col?

'Which?'

'Good. The "good" in "in good hands"?'

'Lawful,' Harpur said.

'That's the kind of proposition you and most of the press can understand, isn't it, Col?'

'What?'

'That the law should be lawful. I'll admit it would be hard to argue against that. Myself, Harpur, being who I am, and of the status and responsibility I hold, I have to look beyond that simple-minded exercise in repetition, in tautology. I have to ask, and go on asking, have they chosen rightly in deciding what is lawful and what is not? Should trading in the commodities be regarded as criminal? Now, you'll no doubt respond with, What does "rightly" mean in that statement: "have they chosen rightly?"?'

'What does "rightly" mean in that statement: "have they chosen rightly?", sir?'

'This, clearly, is the supreme and abiding question, Harpur,' Iles replied.

'And the answer is, is it, sir, does it do *rightly* by – i.e. is it fair to – Ralphy Ember and Manse Shale and their hearty affection for the coke and mainline industry, which, of course, currently at least, is *un*lawful throughout GB?'

Iles drove the Toyota into the Fonton nick's underground parking.

TWENTY-TWO

Harpur saw at once that the ACC didn't have much interest in the opening part of the interrogation. Despite the death, he'd regard it as routine, chickenfeed crime. In line with his habit when bored, he spent a lot of the time stroking his Adam's apple. This was not because he felt fond of it, or got turned on by it. He hated it, despised it and was probably hoping that one day, when he put his hand on it like this, he'd find it had somehow become not quite so sinewy, knobbly and jutting. He wanted a smooth, perfect line between his chin and his chest. Although, of course, he knew that Adam's apples were predominantly a male feature, he said that he didn't want his masculinity to depend on this jagged bundle.

He was bound to accept that the interrogation must deal with early material, but he'd be waiting for Waverton's arrival in the Binnacle story. As Iles had said, he was focused on Waverton and, above all, where Waverton might lead. Did he set up Sandicott Terrace and, if so, where did the orders come from? Whoever gave them was probably still around somewhere, just as Waverton was still around here. This might mean danger continued; danger on the assistant chief's own cherished territory once more and aimed this time at a local figure whom Iles had a satisfactory, delicate business arrangement with: Manse Shale.

These amassed circumstances were sure to infuriate Iles. He would fiercely concentrate on stopping any further threats to the city's precious serenity and healthy, shady commerce. Yes, focus. He would focus. And when Iles focused, he focused hard. His attention to his Adam's apple entailed a kind of focus, but this could be displaced by other, urgent topics. The Adam's apple would always be there for him to come back to. That was the fucking trouble.

Harpur had picked his best interviewer for this rave knifing job, Inspector Caroline Elms. She was a plump, chummy-seeming, round-faced, jolly-looking, thirty-year-old, today in black cord trousers, a blue roll-neck sweater and large, pink-framed, Dame Edna type glasses. She might have been an optician advertising a new, playful style by wearing it. The glasses gave her a jokey, harmless appearance. Caroline could make her voice gossipy, mild, seemingly off-hand. Those she interrogated felt relaxed, and she knew how to cash in on this. Caroline had a brain and memory not much short of the assistant chief's. No need for soft-cop, hard-cop tactics. Her warm, matey-cop approach usually worked OK solo.

She got the mathematics boy from Berwick-on-Tweed, Lance Williamson Dite, to describe his relationship with the disputed girl. He said it had been on-off for nearly a year. That was how relationships tended to fluctuate at his age, she said. It had been the same for her when younger, she told him. Harpur didn't know whether that was right or just a reassuring ploy. Caroline asked about Dite's drugs intake on the night. Answer: grass only.

'One thing puzzles me, Lance: how come you had a knife?' Why had he brought it to a music do?

Because music dos could sometimes turn nasty, he said.

'Yes, I suppose not all music soothes the savage breast,' Caroline said. 'Some of it *turned* people savage. Think of the Nazis' love of Wagner. You brought the knife for protection, did you, Lance?'

'Yes, for protection,' he said.

'I think we have to try to work out how this purpose – protection, self-defence – became an attack instead?' she replied.

A solicitor had been drafted in to take care of Dite and he objected to this. Harpur expected it. Caroline probably did, too. It was a try-on, a leading question. Perhaps in 50 per cent of cases she'd get away with such venerable trickery. But perhaps the lawyer was familiar with her methods. He said the question assumed Dite's action *was* an attack, whereas he might have been trying only to safeguard himself. That would be consistent with what he had just said.

'But the stabbed man, Wyn Normanton Vaughan, was unarmed,' Caroline said gently, and with a puzzled, homely smile.

'My client would not be sure of that at the time,' Kopner,

the solicitor, said. 'He has told us he knew this type of evening could turn nasty. "Nasty" might mean knives.'

Harpur saw that Caroline was fishing for evidence of preparation, of calculation, of intent: the *mens rea* – guilty mind – as the Latin-loving law manuals for police trainees would put it. Not a pushover. There was no known connection between Dite and Vaughan before the Binnacle night.

Caroline asked now about what she called 'the preliminary skirmish'. Iles became more tense, more 'focused' on what was being said, rather than his neck. Harpur could understand why: something preliminary meant there must be something subsequent, didn't it? This development would be why Iles had felt compelled to come to a distant fragment of his empire and sit with Harpur on straight-backed, kitchen-type chairs near the door of number 2A Interview, Recording and Video Room. He could have stayed at headquarters and viewed proceedings on a screen. But, clearly, Iles wanted to be bodily present; and possibly to put some questions to Dite himself. The ACC liked participation; and so those attempts to take over funerals, for instance. Talking with Harpur not long ago, Iles had mentioned that 'pro-active' was his second name.

Caroline guided Dite through the moments when he first realized his girlfriend, Avril, had disappeared, her return with Vaughan, and then the shouting, cursing, pushing, incompetent punching, and the split into two opposed factions. Dite was short, thin, his dark hair already showing strands of grey. He wore a denim jacket over a black vest, jeans, scuffed black shoes.

'No knife at this stage,' Caroline said. 'How did you conceal it, Lance?'

Kopner stirred again and seemed about to protest. This question took for granted Dite's possession of a knife. But the lawyer must have decided there was no sane reason to query it and he stayed silent. The defence was going to be not that Dite had no knife, and therefore couldn't have stabbed anyone, but that he'd brought it in case he had to look after himself. He'd believed he was doing that when he killed Vaughan. Or so he'd be advised to claim.

Caroline said, 'Most males had on T-shirts and jeans. Did you wear the jacket because it could accommodate the sheathed knife out of sight?' A jacket to carry the weapon could be more proof of preparedness, calculation and intent, but that point had already been conceded and Kopner let this go now, also.

Caroline said, 'And then someone from outside the two battle groups arrived – a man older than any of you and he tried to calm things, yes? He scared you, perhaps. We now know him to be Frank Louis Waverton, possibly present as a supplier of gear, or foreman and escort of some suppliers. At any rate, not present to rave.'

'He told us to cool it,' Dite said. 'He worried in case trouble spread and buggered up trading. Maybe he was on a percentage. His clothes looked pricey. He might need the cash.'

'Did he frighten you?'

'He was big. He had that way with him.'

'Which?' Caroline said.

'Sort of no messing with him. Professional.'

'Professional what?'

'Crook. Heavy.'

'What did he say?'

'He said to stop pissing around, he had a business to run. Along those lines but with more swearing.'

'You can unveil the words. I'll have heard them before, I expect. If not, there's a dictionary in one of the drawers.'

'He said, stop pissing around and chuck the fucking aggro, he had a fucking business to run.' Dite gave a slight shrug, as if to say Caroline had asked for it and so there it was, verbatim, expletives undeleted.

'Was there any response to that?' Caroline said.

'Someone said, like, "It's not *your* business, is it? You're no baron, only here because you've been sent by Shale or Ralphy Ember. You're just a worker." Yes, "just a worker", that was the phrase, like destroying his pomp.'

'Who said it?'

'A guy I didn't know, still don't know.'

'Undergraduate?'

'Most likely. About that age and cheek.'

'Any reply?'

'"I am who I am," the man said. Waverton? Was that the name you gave?'

'Yes, Frank Louis Waverton,' Caroline said.

'Right.'

'Was there more?'

'He said, "And you'll do what I tell you or you won't get out of this place in recognizable form".'

'"I am who I am"?' Caroline said. 'Blimey.'

'Yes, like God in the Old Testament. After that, things went quiet, except for the music. Then he spoke again. He became very mild-voiced and threatening: "Anything in my way, I remove it. You're in my way, laddy, if there's more stupidity".'

'Then what?'

'He went back to where he was before and stood near one of the dealers.'

'Then what?'

'Someone said we were rubbish and yellow for listening to him when he was only a dirty spy and a stinking traitor.'

Iles grunted. It might have been involuntary excitement that the topic had been reached at last. It might have been a terse signal to Caroline to dig for more in this area. That was how she seemed to react. Caroline might be clever enough to pick up this unspoken order from the assistant chief. 'Who said that?' she asked.

'About being a spy?'

'Yes?'

'I didn't know him, either. And then others said the same kind of thing. The music was still back at top volume so it was hard to keep track of what was going on – what people were saying – but some did seem to agree with that stuff about the spying, like some of them had heard rumours involving this Waverton. There are always rumours in the drugs scene – the companies are known about, naturally: Ember's, Shale's, and the choice they offer.'

'And the fighting, did it restart now?'

'Some shoving and snarling, but nothing bad, not straight away. Customary. There was another break in the music. The first guy – the one who said Waverton was only a worker – he . . .'

Dite hesitated. He glanced about the room as though reluctant to let the recording and filming machines make permanent what he would say now.

'Look, you're not going to like this,' he said. 'I ought to tell you in advance.'

'More swearing? Try me,' Caroline replied.

'This first guy says, "Cover-up. It's bloody obvious."'

'What cover-up?' Caroline said.

'Police cover-up.'

'Covering up what?'

'The situation.'

'Which?'

'The murder of the woman and the boy in the ambush.'

'He was suggesting a link to that? Mrs Shale and her stepson, Laurent?'

'Right. It's the kind of gossip around, I gather. This first guy shouts that the gunman in the ambush got wiped out, and no inquiries beyond, to do with, like, who sent him? Someone big, powerful, a super-villain looking to spread, to expand. Money involved? Money at a high level?'

'What did he mean by that – a high pile of money?'

'It might be a high pile of money, but he meant the money must have gone to a high level . . . I told you you wouldn't like this – he meant money to a high level in the police, to someone, or more than one, who could control things and make sure the investigation didn't press further than the hired hitman, a nobody, a violence flunky.'

'Did he have information about this?'

'I don't know. It's what he said. The music kicked in again and there's hardly any more talk. Some people from both the groups drift off to dance.'

'Which music?' Caroline asked.

'Some of the group's own stuff, but Bahamas-style,' he said.

'Like "Bitter Memories"?' Iles asked.

'Sort of, yes,' Dite said. He glanced over to Iles, surprised at the interruption.

'Yet real fun in some Bahamas numbers,' Iles said. 'Not all bitter memories.'

'No,' Dite said. 'And then, suddenly, I see this guy who'd been in the toilets with Avril coming at me, crouched but moving fast, his eyes mad and full of hate. People got out of his way, gave him a path direct to me. They were scared. Oh,

I should have said Avril was with me again. She'd come back, as if it had all been nothing with this Vaughan guy. But it was like he wanted her and would get rid of me if I tried to stop him. There'd be no sense trying to talk to him. He was beyond that.'

'And so you pull the knife?' Caroline said.

'It's as you said earlier. I had on this denim jacket with an inside pocket. I could get at it fast.'

Kopner said, 'He'd anticipated possible trouble and had to be able to reach his protective weapon quickly. This explains the jacket. Probably illegal to be carrying the chiv, but under-standable.'

'Three blows,' Caroline said.

'He seemed to be coming on after the first two,' Dite said.

'Two were deep chest wounds, very near the heart,' Caroline said. 'He could still move?'

'I hadn't stopped him.'

'He's very close, yes? Didn't you see at this late point that he was unarmed?' Caroline asked

'But by this stage my client was committed,' Kopner said. 'He had to make himself and Avril safe.'

'And Waverton? Where was he?' Caroline asked

'I didn't notice. I don't know whether he tried to intervene again,' Dite said.

'If he did it didn't work, did it?' Caroline said.

'That's extremely uncalled for,' Kopner said.

'I don't mind a bit of high-mindedness and piety from a lawyer now and then, Kopner,' Iles replied. 'I can assure you I don't find it in the least nauseating. I'm glad to place this on record. You're absolutely entitled to use any kind of tactics to get yourself ahead of the prosecution. I thought that aggrieved comment from you came over as brilliantly heartfelt and sincere. Many would accept it for what it sought to be. Congratulations!'

Iles got up and walked towards Caroline and Dite where they sat one on each side of a small table. There was a carafe of water on it and a couple of glasses.

The ACC stood alongside Dite. 'So, Vaughan on the floor, blood a-plenty, kids trying to stop the flow with garments folded to make pads, I expect. Mouth-to-mouth, anyone? But you don't remember whether Waverton returned to see what had happened?'

'There would be inevitable confusion,' Kopner said.

'Things are a blur from the time I saw him coming at me and I went for the knife,' Dite replied.

'To protect yourself,' Kopner said.

'To protect myself,' Dite said.

'*Un*blur them,' Iles said.

'I don't think he was there,' Dite replied.

'He'd got clear, bailed out, had he?' Iles said. 'Despite the din he might have heard people calling him a two-timing accessory before the fact to a murder, another murder, a double murder of totally harmless people. His street-cred, rave-cred, had gone. A necessary fast exit.'

'Speculation,' Kopner said.

'Got anything better?' Iles replied.

TWENTY-THREE

The Vaughan murder had taken place too late at night to figure in the city's morning newspaper but Harpur had seen and heard television and radio reports of the death before he set out with Iles after a couple hours' sleep to the Fonton interrogation. Denise had done an extensive fried breakfast for them – two eggs each, one sausage each, bacon, mushrooms, black pudding – and then driven the children to school in her Fiat, on her way to a lecture later at the university.

By midday television had a full bulletin locally and on the national networks covering the Binnacle violence. When the interrogation session had ended and Dite was taken back to the cells, Harpur and Iles stayed on alone in the room and watched the BBC TV news on Harpur's phone. He knew that evening newspapers would pick up the story, and tomorrow's dailies in the morning. Media editors adored this kind of tale, and especially television editors. He could imagine their whooped reaction: 'Lavish pleasure turning to tragedy, symbolic touches as to the way we live now, some of us, with good visuals!'

The central good visual in this tale was the Binnacle itself and the setting: the beach, the two uninhabited Nivot tidal islands, and the sea. The Binnacle retained some of its original handsomeness and distinction, but was obviously tumbling into decay, neglected, unrepaired, battered by coastal storms, abused by vandals, commandeered by ravers and drug dealers, and further debased by a sordid, pothead knifing.

Yes, the place had symbolism. The editors wouldn't bother to define very closely even to themselves what exactly the symbolism was, but it clearly had to do with the termination of one-time classy and privileged leisure and a steep slide into . . . into something else; no need to define that, either; no way of doing that without sounding corny, square and snobbish. Not good for ratings; the way we live now would cover it.

Harpur half-wished Denise was with him. He had an idea
that the Shakespeare play, *Romeo and Juliet*, contained
stabbings caused by girls or a girl and he would have liked to
check if the Binnacle disaster had some similar incidents.
Instead of Denise, Harpur mentioned the possible comparison
to Iles.

'Yes,' the ACC said, 'but sloping off to the lavs for whatever
purpose is a uniquely modern touch.'

The television teams must have arrived pretty soon after
dawn. There were still some ravers hanging about. Vaughan's
body had been removed but the screening tent remained in place
and the camera could linger on that while the reporter gave her
terse account of the fatality. Then the camera roamed about
inside what she called 'the one-time banqueting hall, now, for
one night, a dance floor', showing torn, drooping wallpaper,
fragments of broken furniture, the lower panels of double doors
to what had been the kitchens kicked through, the mahogany
banister to stairs leading down from the bar torn from its rails
and lying among brick and glass debris on the floor.

'This is atmosphere, Col,' Iles said. 'This is poignancy. This
is mutability.' The pictures enthralled him. Concern about
his Adam's apple got relegated.

The television reporter talked to Francis Garland and to
eyewitnesses.

(a) Garland:

He gave what Harpur recognized, of course, as the formal
account in the formula language of formal accounts. 'I can
confirm that a twenty-year-old male died from knife wounds
after an altercation at an illegal dancing event, or so-called
"rave", here, at the former Binnacle Hotel, in the early hours
of this morning. The dead male has not been officially identified
but is thought to be Wyn Normanton Vaughan, a third-year
undergraduate at the city's university, and to come from Brecon,
Powys, Wales. On the assumption that this identification is
correct Wyn Normanton Vaughan's parents have been informed.
It is understood they are on holiday in Australia and will return
as soon as possible.

'The reason for the altercation is not at this stage clear but police are considering all possibilities. A male undergraduate from Berwick-on-Tweed, also aged twenty, has been arrested on suspicion of murder. Witnesses to the disturbance are helping officers with their inquiries, which will be on-going through the day, and beyond if necessary. No charges have been made.

'We believe there were two stages to the incident. A disagreement arose and scuffling between two groups ensued. No weapons were used at this point. A middle-aged man who was present intervened and seemed able to restore calm. But shortly afterwards the disturbance recommenced and quickly developed into an affray during which Wyn Normanton Vaughan received several knife wounds to the upper body and fell to the floor. Some of those nearby tried first aid and an ambulance was called. It arrived within fifteen minutes. Paramedics gave further treatment but at 3.55 a.m. he was declared dead at the scene.'

(b) Lorna Pettigrew (driving instructor):

'At first it was just like the sort of squabble that sometimes happens at raves of this kind – boys showing off, being Mr Hardman, that sort of thing, you know? It could have been about a girl. Not me! No, no, no. A sort of jealousy thing. It's always a possible when you get crowds and music, most people a bit high, like.

'Then what seemed to be a real Mr Hardman, older, hefty, bossy came and told them to get sensible, not to behave like twirps. Some swearing: "fucking" this and that. Rage. He made them sound sort of juvenile – schoolchildren scrapping in the playground. It seemed to work. Like calm came. Some people went back to the dancing and so on. But a few seemed to know this Mr Hardman. They had a name – Waverton? Frank Waverton?'

(c) Harry Brightman (postman, Lorna's friend):

'Yes, Waverton. A few seemed to recognize him. That would be from other gigs, I should think. They did seem to know about a bad side to him, a dark side. Some said – not said, yelled – some shouted he shouldn't be able to tell people how to behave. The roughhouse began again and then . . . and then the knife and all this.'

(d) Garland:

'We will be talking to Mr Waverton and others.'

In the interrogation room, watching all this on the minor screen, Iles said, 'Not sure I like that, Col.'

'What, sir?'

'Implications here, Harpur.'

'Which?'

'In some ways a plus, I'll concede that.'

'Which?'

'These kids, mouthing the accusations against him.'

'Of treachery?'

'Of treachery. They are kids who might be users, Well, no "might" about it. They certainly *are* users. And so they pick up talk inside the drugs scene, including these suspicions about Waverton. This is one of the reasons we're here for the interrogation, isn't it, Col? They speak the kind of information I'm looking for. This is a considerable plus.'

'We can't say "information", sir. Rumour.'

'Why I stress rumour from *inside* the trade. And it comes from more than one voice. This is substantial, Harpur, very high-grade rumour, bordering on the undeniable.'

'Possibly. It might be more than one voice but with the same wobbly source.'

'Don't undervalue rumour, Col. Who was it said history was just a distillation of rumour?'

'I'm always getting asked that, sir,' Harpur replied.

'I *need* these rumours to be right, Harpur, absolutely *need* them to be right. But you will answer in your honest, cramped, banal, unimaginative way, what I *need* is not the same as what *is*.'

'What you *need*, sir, is not the same as what *is*,' Harpur replied.

'You mean, "Oh, reason not the need"?'

'Someone else said that?'

'We're having a Shakespeare session, Col.'

'He definitely had a way with words. This has been noted by all sorts, at home and abroad. And so *many words*, some totally spot-on, which is why they've come down through the ages. The ability with words is known as a "facility". I mean those words came easily to him. He didn't need to be looking them up to check. We should all be very pleased with William Shakespeare. Ideas never stopped coming to him, and he was willing to share them with the population via plays.'

'Did you ever think of becoming an English literature don at Oxford, Harpur?'

'As a matter of fact, I've always fancied an evening at one of those piggish, pissed-as-a-fart dinners called gaudies.'

'Waverton's name – the mentions,' Iles replied. 'This is the debit side, the peril side of Binnacle. His name is networked. The national papers will have more on him tomorrow. People who hired Frank Waverton to plan Sandicott Terrace won't be happy to hear several of those kids felt there was something wrong with him, something secret and dubious.'

'We don't *know* he had any involvement in Sandicott, sir, although you might *need* to know he did. After all, Waverton is still working for Manse Shale. Is that likely if he's suspected of betrayal? You mentioned *The Godfather* quote about keeping your enemies closer than your friends, but I'm not so sure.'

'Fucking touché, Col, or re-touché. No, we don't *know* and probably Manse doesn't *know,* either. He might be waiting for confirmation before he acts. Shale is like that – scrupulous in his own fashion, unhurried. But, although we don't *know* in italics, we can wonder. We can intelligently, or even inspiration-ally, wonder. True, Lorna and Harry didn't seem clear on what was dubious about Waverton, but some of Garland's other witnesses might spell out the traitorous side.'

'*Possibly* traitorous.'

'Those who hired him . . . all right, Harpur, *if* they hired him, if they did, they will not feel good about his being grilled by police.'

'Grilled? He's only a witness to a student death. He's not accused, sir.'

'Yes, that's how it might start – a witness interview. But he's going to be asked why these kids dismissed his warning – what they meant when a couple of them bellowed about the treachery.'

'*Possible* treachery.'

'This is the kind of interview liable to go off in any direction, Col. It can start about one, specific, apparently limited topic, but follow new revelations that arise totally unplanned. That risk of fresh disclosures would be enough to scare the big-timer he acted for – the major schemer somewhere, who ordered the ambush to get rid of Shale so as to grab his firm, but in fact got rid of Mrs Shale and Laurent, through ghastly error.'

Harpur said, 'You think Waverton's in danger because of the Binnacle and media publicity? You believe someone will want to make sure he doesn't talk about those other, wider matters when interviewed?'

'Possibly, Col, if I might pinch one of your theme words, yours personally, not Shakespeare's. Those "other wider matters" are what intrigue me, Naomi and Laurent Shale murdered in the Jag are "those other wider matters", Harpur. I don't want Waverton dead before he has a chance to do some divulging.'

'He might not have anything to divulge about those other, wider matters, sir. His walk-on part at the Binnacle might be his total role.'

'Two "mights" and I'll add another, Col, and a "maybe". That "might be" his total role, yes. Or maybe not.'

TWENTY-FOUR

Rose Waverton, watched the morning TV news bulletin after seeing Olive off on the school bus. Rose felt uneasy. 'We will be talking to Mr Waverton and others.' She didn't like this final reply to the reporter from a top-rank cop in charge of the Binnacle aftermath. In fact, she'd disliked, also, what went before it in the channel's account of the violence: those chatty prats playing about carelessly, vindictively with Frank's name. 'Waverton? Frank Waverton?' 'Yes, Waverton.' Her surname, too, of course: she felt as though she'd been edged into something foul.

The pay-off line really troubled her. She heard a threat there: 'We will be talking to Mr Waverton.' It came over as a sort of crowing: 'Oh, yes, indeed, we'll certainly be talking to Mr Waverton!' Forget the 'and others'. The lawman seemed to promise a spotlight especially for Frank. Rose considered this unwanted, and possibly dangerous.

Frank had been late home and was still in bed asleep. This gave her time to think about the possible results of the Binnacle disaster, and, above all, about the possible results of media publicity, national and local; that deeply inconvenient, intrusive spotlight.

For God's sake, why did Frank have to get himself entangled in those grotesque hostilities? Had he switched off his brain, his instinct for self-preservation? It sounded as though he thought the quarrel might badly affect business that night at the hotel. Well, business wasn't something holy and due continuous protection. He could have – should have – stayed out of the sick brawling. She rethought this. The kind of business he was in could definitely not be regarded as holy. But it did require protection. What he did at the Binnacle, though, wasn't the way to give it that protection.

The point was, wasn't it, that if Frank had helped set up a catastrophic ambush at Sandicott Terrace, the people who'd recruited him to do it, persuaded him, purchased him, would not wish to have Frank under intensive questioning by police now. 'We will be talking to Mr Waverton.' What that meant, though, was: 'We will be *listening* to Mr Waverton. We will be digging in deep to Mr Waverton.'

On the face of it, those discussions would concern a fatal quarrel at the Binnacle rave, with Frank as simply a witness, a well-intentioned, peace-loving witness, who'd done a sort of policing job. Yes, on the face of it. But there could be an alarming link now between that killing and the chaotic deaths of Manse Shale's second wife and son. This was how Frank had come to feature in the early section of the TV news item, those reported shouted comments by some of the ravers. Would Olive get rough, snide questions at school about her father, now his name had been broadcast as part of that very unpleasant tale?

Rose had still never asked Frank head-on whether the rumours about his role in the cruel Sandicott mess-up were accurate. She didn't want to provoke lies from him – a version of the Kay and Michael *Godfather* confrontation. Sometimes Rose considered life imitated films, not the other way about. A big lie, if one day exposed, would taint their marriage for as long as the marriage lasted. The suspicion that he might be lying was already threatening her feelings for him.

And what if Frank admitted involvement in the Sandicott attack? Oh, God, that would bring an appalling truth for her to swallow: her husband had helped engineer the deaths of two innocents, a woman and a child. OK, they were executed by mistake. But if he'd helped create the conditions for that mistake she would surely find it monstrous, unforgivable, as though he'd gone into partnership with a frighteningly twisted, malignant Fate. He'd be ghastly evidence that men and women might scheme and plan but unscheduled events could make all their effort null and preposterous. It would gravely diminish him in her eyes; he wasn't only traitorous, he was abominably jinxed, a pathetic, accidental blight.

Did that mean she could have tolerated his treachery if it had led to the slaughter of the right person, Manse Shale, not his wife and son? This idea disturbed her badly. How could she believe betrayal was OK as long as it worked efficiently? Hell!

And now another seemingly unrelated crisis might reach out and put a further curse on Frank – the Binnacle, and a death wholly unconnected to him except that loud-mouth druggies at the Binnacle had enforced the connection. 'Waverton? Frank Waverton?' 'Yes, Waverton.' He had actually tried to stop the feuding that produced an awful finale, yet it was this unnecessary, foolish intervention that put his name on show, perhaps turned himself into a target.

Rose had done some reading and thought these sorts of random setbacks and unexpected perils amounted to what one set of philosophers used to call the 'absurd'. As she judged it, for them this word had signified more than idiotic and daft. It suggested that apparently haphazard incidents were always liable to barge in and casually smash men's arrangements, show them to be laughably doomed.

The so-called existentialist thinkers were supposed to combat this terrible, malign chanciness by doggedly accepting responsibility for their own individual lives. Fight back! Rose had never been able to understand this last bit. You could accept responsibility for your selfhood, yes, but then get clobbered and clobbered again by the endless 'absurdities' of the world, so that accepting responsibility became a kind of self-cancelling nonsense, because it was obvious you *couldn't* be responsible. Life's contrariwise, vindictively mischievous elements stifled that hope. No wonder someone said the only credible ploy to counter the world's cavalier, heartless hostilities was suicide. She thought this kind of constant, predatory, destructive absurdity had made Frank a special victim, and she wasn't confident he could handle it well, or at all.

But Rose wasn't a philosopher and knew it. She could get lost in that hocus pocus fog. In any case, there would usually come a time in Rose's reading and thinking when she'd get fed up with the waffle and flannel shipped to her mind by books, and she would long for something concrete, definite, non-intellectual, anti-intellectual, straightforward, simple, physically touchable.

Sandicott Terrace would do. She drove there, but *en route* still thinking hard. She knew she read a lot, without any system or special purpose and picked up plenty of ideas, some of them possibly all right, some of them possibly not. She'd discovered recently that her kind of slapdash approach to reading could be called 'desultory'. And, during her desultory reading she'd come across an essay by Charles Lamb about the pleasures of desultory reading, and so her desultory reading had guided her somehow to a term for what she was up to in her desultory fashion without actually knowing it was desultory.

Yes, some of what she read could be correct, some not. And what she made of it could, similarly, be correct or not. For instance, what she read could be out of date. Perhaps current philosophers would find totally absurd that notion of the absurd.

Rose had thought of taking a photograph of Frank with her to Sandicott Terrace, but then decided against. It would seem like pre-judging him. Her aim was to talk to some householders there and ask if, shortly before the blasting of the Jaguar, they saw anyone carrying out some sort of survey of the location, particularly the junction of Sandicott Terrace and Landau Road.

Naturally, she realized the police had probably made those sorts of inquiry immediately after the shootings. Naturally, she also knew that if someone wanted to pick a good spot for an interception there would be no need actually to go there. This could probably be better done from a street map. But she needed contact with the bricks and mortar facts, and with the ordinary, alert, observant people of the neighbourhood.

As far as she could remember from gossip and media coverage, the Jaguar, with Naomi Shale at the wheel, had lurched up on to the pavement in Sandicott Terrace when she was shot and lost control. The car knocked down a stretch of low wall around the front garden of one of the houses and then stopped. The damage had been repaired now but she could identify the house from a slight difference in the colour of the brickwork halfway along. This was what a mind ought to do – distinguish between different stretches of brick, very touchable brick, not flap about with existentialism.

She'd left her car about a hundred metres back and walked past the house and up to the junction with the wider Landau Road, a main drag. She had to wonder if she was traipsing over ground that Frank might have traipsed over, but with sharper purpose: a reconnaissance ahead of murder.

Rose thought she could see why someone might fancy this spot as ideal for an ambush. The Jaguar coming along Sandicott Terrace must have been slowing as it approached the junction. For several seconds, while Naomi and the children passed, the Jag would have been very close to any vehicle parked on the left side of the terrace, just before the stop sign at the join with Landau. It had been close enough for the gunman to riddle the Jaguar, but apparently not close enough for him to see he had the wrong target or targets.

The jumpiness, the tension, must have shoved him into deciding he'd been clearly and specifically ordered to hit a Jaguar at about this spot and this time, so he'd hit a Jaguar, never mind who was in it. Maybe he was a novice at car murder, lacking cool, too hasty for precision. She remembered, didn't she, that he'd been operating from a silver Mondeo? He was killed not very long afterwards and before he could tell who sent him.[7]

An elderly woman came out from the house with the reconstituted wall and stood on the small slice of lawn behind.

'Hello there, m'dear, you seem uncertain – pacing about. But, yes, this is, indeed, the location,' she said.

'I've heard about it. I came out of interest,' Rose replied.

'Are you more police? I don't think so. It's too long after now, isn't it? What's left to discover?'

'Just out of interest,' Rose said.

'Many an officer we had here and hereabouts then, some in uniform, some plain clothes. This was a considerable incident. Sandicott debouching into Landau became what might be called a nexus.'

'Certainly.'

'Not minor police. As I said, considerable. Very fine smooth uniform, one of them. Iles. He was here several times. That kind of high-quality cloth speaks of leadership, of command, Underlings recognize this, respond to it, in automatic obeisance. That kind of cloth is of a similarity with Napoleon's famous three-cornered hat denoting supremo status.'

'I think I've heard of Iles.'

---

[7] See *I Am Gold*

'Any roosts to be ruled he rules them. That's what my hubby says about him. But Iles could be civil with it now and then. He saw to the wall. Quite spontaneous.'

'The replacement?'

'This wall has a message for us, being struck by the Jaguar when bullets had finished off proper steering, no blame to the lady driver whatsoever. This wall halted the Jaguar, but also some of it collapsed. Civilization is similarly fragile. On the other hand some walls definitely should come down, such as the one between West and East Germany. This was a wall whose removal enhanced civilization.

'But most probably you'll be thinking of the Psalmist, "By my God have I leaped over a wall."' She had a small chuckle and gave a couple of nods, as if to agree with Rose's unspoken Bible reference. 'Well, the Jaguar couldn't do that, of course, but the harm wasn't serious. Iles gave immediate instructions as to rebuilding. I'll ask you to inspect it.'

Perhaps she recognized Rose's need. 'It's an exemplary wall,' she said. She bent and passed her hand over part of it. Touchable bricks, no question, she thought.

'The wall is as good as new,' the woman said. 'Well, better than, since some of it has suffered no wear and tear. That's not to say we didn't worry about the deaths. No muttering to ourselves "it's an ill wind", a maxim. A bit of wall is nothing compared to all the blood and pain. That Iles panjandrum, already mentioned, could not have been more upset. Usually, looking at him, his face and so on, you might get the notion he didn't give a monkey's about anyone, dead or alive. This is the kind of face they're taught in the top police colleges to have, known as judicial. Most probably they'd have lectures with mirrors in front of them learning how to look like eternal frost.

'But Iles could also manage something different. He had his head in through the broken window of that Jag, obviously stricken by the awful awfulness of it, and the little girl cowering yet brave. If you come across him when he's not in the gorgeous blue uniform but civvy garb, you'll be able tell him from his Adam's apple. Prominent. Mountainous.'

'I thought to myself as I stepped towards the stop sign that this must have been a carefully chosen piece of ground for the attack,' Rose said. 'There are geographical and architectural pluses.'

'You said you were not police, did you?'

'Yes. I'm not police.'

'That was a police sort of question – about the chosen ground, regarding tactical features.'

'It was simply a thought that came at me out of nowhere, as it were, when I stood at the junction.'

'The junction was important, no doubt of it. A traffic confluence as is generally the case with junctions. "This junction has capabilities", as that famous garden expert in the eighteenth century might have said.'

'It's the choice of it that fascinates me,' Rose replied. 'The opting.'

'But why, if you're not police?'

'Curiosity, I suppose.'

'People do get like that about crimes – curiosity. It's a sign of interest in how the crooked mind works, because, inherently, of course, we're all human and might be capable of the same kind of lawlessness if we didn't keep the, so to speak, lid on it. No harm in wondering about this. You and I, we might look at a junction and see a mere junction, whereas the villain would possibly regard it as a kind of no-man's land, to be utilized for an advantage.' She was short, sturdy, cheerful looking and Rose would guess in her seventies. She wore a turquoise cardigan over a floral-print dress.

A man of about her age and height came out and stood with her on the grass, like a couple advertising joyfully comfortable retirement homes. He was long-faced, thin-to-spare, tame-voiced. He had on what seemed to be trousers from a navy, pinstripe suit and a black crew-neck sweater.

'I guessed you were having one of your *al fresco* conversations, love,' he said, 'apropos the incident of less than blessed memory.'

'This lady has been re-living the moments out of plain, general curiosity, not forensically,' the woman said. 'I've mentioned the nexus, debouching and the confluence.'

'We're used to such visitors, aren't we, Doreen?' he said. 'This property has come to resemble a depot or a hide for discreetly observing wild life. Perhaps she'd like to come in for a cup of tea, iced or conventional. We are very aware of preferences, respect them. A choice between iced tea and conventional might seem a trivial distinction and in some senses it certainly is, but we'd rather regard it as typifying Choice with a capital C signalling a general climate of free will.'

'Thank you, but I must be getting along,' Rose said. 'However, what I wondered, as a way of understanding this violence, was whether you had noted anyone pre the attack sort of mentally mapping the set-up here, the potential of the locale to become an execution scene.'

'Many have asked us that I think it's fair to report, isn't it, Doreen, amateur and professional?'

'Undoubtedly,' Doreen said. 'The nexus aspect.'

'This is a kind of hindsight question, if I might use that term,' he told Rose. 'It's the answer we've always given when similarly asked, so don't feel offended or brushed off, please. Glancing from the window into Sandicott and up to Landau one might have seen folk going this way or that on foot, but they wouldn't really be of note at that time – not until the shooting had taken place and caused the area and those moving about in it to become of possible importance, a *post hoc* judgement rather than *pre*. This is why I name your line of thought "hindsight". It would be very strange and presumptuous to glance at one of these people as he, or indeed she, walked through Sandicott to Landau or vice versa and decide this was clearly a person preparing things for a fusillade against a top-of-the-range Jag. Nobody was going to produce a gun and practise some pop-shotting. The time in question is so far back now that the pre-assault scene or scenes, is or are an unrecoverable entity or entities. To my way of thinking, that is.'

'Graham has a way of summing things up,' Doreen said. 'It's what might without overstatement be designated a flair. Many have remarked on it in a favourable, even admiring, manner. He was a carpet-layer for many years concerned with all kinds and sizes of floors and stairs. Show Graham a Stanley knife and he'll become very reminiscent. There were tricky, tucked away corners to get the carpet into if wall-to-wall. And the necessity that doors could open over the carpet without ruffling it up.'

'One of the reasons I came to Sandicott today was to talk to ordinary people,' Rose said. 'But you two are so ordinary it goes beyond the ordinary – all that obvious stuff about hindsight and junctions and the ruptured wall.'

'There's a film called that,' Graham replied excitedly. 'It comes on TV.'

'Called what?' Rose asked.

'*Ordinary People*,' he said. 'It's labelled ironic in viewing guides. This indicates that the title should be taken as the opposite of what the film *is*. You couldn't have a movie genuinely about ordinary people as it would be so fucking ordinary and dull, making tea or treating the dog's distemper. No, it's about ordinary people stuck into events that are not ordinary at all, and the way the supposedly ordinary people deal with these events makes them very different from ordinary and therefore, in the movie, OK for Mary Tyler Moore and Donald Sutherland to star as.'

'You think you're like that, do you?' Rose said.

'If you were a Hollywood producer you couldn't go to actors like Moore and Sutherland and ask, "Can you do ordinary?"' Graham replied. 'They'd be insulted for one of two reasons: first because you weren't sure they had the ability; and, second, because you thought they were so bloody wooden that they'd be super-suited to lifeless parts.'

'You're down here to see if you can discover whether someone you know, someone who might be dear to you, came to Sandicott–Landau to decide if it was a suitable slice of terrain for a killing, aren't you?' Doreen said. 'This purpose radiates from you. The wall and brickwork don't really grab you as topics, do they? And I very strongly doubt that you were considering the Psalms re the wall. That was merry-making only on my part, wasn't it?'

'I *like* the bricks,' Rose said.

'There's a rumour around, isn't there, that someone called Waverton, Frank Waverton, was the one who did the exploration?' Doreen replied. 'This came out at the Binnacle ding-dong and in tittle-tattle before that. Possibly he's your boyfriend or even husband. You look the sort who would have a husband. Sort of perturbed.'

'Is your name Waverton?' Graham asked.

'I believe you've both turned against me since I declined the conventional or iced tea,' Rose replied. 'A drastically changed tone. Unfriendly bordering on the antagonistic.'

'You said you had to get along and yet you're still here,' Doreen replied. 'Simply you didn't want to take tea with Gray and me. Your rejection of the offer was sodding churlish and hurtful, you blasé twat. Graham is a great believer in good manners. This house, our home, would have been put temporarily at your service. A nose was turned up. Yours.'

'Many conversations seem to be about one matter but in truth have a quite different subject,' he said. 'Things these days are rarely straight.'

'I've told him that among men of his age this is quite normal and there's no point in spending big money at a cock clinic,' Doreen said.

'I really will be getting along now,' Rose replied. 'I have to pick up a takeaway for lunch.'

'It's been delightful talking to you,' Doreen said.

'The bonniest of bon voyages,' Graham said.

TWENTY-FIVE

Although Harpur's daughters didn't think much of the police as a species, Hazel and Jill were often quite kindly and gentle towards him personally and liked to be what they very sincerely considered of assistance in any of his inquiries. Although Jill would admit that some detective work had to be confidential, in general they detested secrecy by Harpur, regarding it as betrayal and as a juvenile wish to know more about some matters than they did. Harpur could see they felt badly snubbed at not hearing about Mrs Waverton's visit to Arthur Street until days after.

There was another visitor now, though, who'd arrived while only the girls were at home. He sensed there'd been a fairly thorough question- and answer-exchange before he returned to the house. Sometimes Harpur wondered whether it was wise to have his name, address and number in the directory. But he knew that police stations – and especially police headquarters – frightened some people: the formality, the bureaucracy, the likely lack of privacy. A chat at 126 Arthur Street could be confidential and one-to-one – unless, that is, Hazel and Jill got to the caller first. It happened only rarely: today, for instance.

'Here's something extremely strange, Dad,' Jill said. 'Denise told us Mrs Rose Waverton came to see you not long ago, didn't she, and now this lady wants to talk to you about someone she thinks *was* Mrs Rose Waverton? Not sure, but most likely. Things that don't seem to be connected at all suddenly turn out to have important links. This house has become a kind of hub.'

'A nexus,' Hazel said.

'A what?' Jill replied.

'Nexus,' Hazel said. 'A drawing together of strands.'

'Of course, I know this lady,' Harpur said. He'd just come in and joined them in the big sitting room. He loved this room now the shelving had been taken down and all Megan's books got rid of except a couple that Jill wanted – *The Sweet Science,*

about boxing, and the *Diaries* of someone who she said wrote
funny plays and got murdered, Joe Orton. She kept them handy
on a mahogany coffee table.

'Yes, of course, of course, you know this lady, Dad,' Hazel
said.

'Most probably you could of met her and talked to her after
the shooting at Sandicott,' Jill said. 'That's where she lives.
Just by the junction with Landau: Mrs Doreen Howells.'

'I wanted to be in touch with Mr Iles,' Doreen Howells said.
'He was so helpful regarding the wall. I thought it would be
nice to show our gratitude by bringing some info.'

'Mrs Howells has spoken to us about the wall,' Jill said. 'I
told her I feel certain Mr Iles would be very swift and urgent
in such wall matters. This would be one of the reasons he
reached the rank of assistant chief. "Very good at walls" should
be on his Personnel Department file.'

'He's like that – decisive,' Hazel said.

'Haze is biased,' Jill said.

'Biased?' Doreen Howells said.

'He used to have a thing about Hazel,' Jill said. 'Sort of
romancing?'

'Cow-viper,' Hazel replied.

'He'd come here with a vermilion scarf on to make himself
look dashing and younger. We did a poem in school about the
young Lord Lochinvar. I think that's who Ilesy fancied himself
as – "so faithful in love, so dauntless in war" – faithful to Haze
not his wife. Dad worried,' Jill said. 'Haze was only a teenager
but Ilesy is forties, grey-haired, married with a kid called Fanny.
When she grows up she won't think that very clever. But Des
Iles stopped sniffing around Haze when he found she had a
special boyfriend near her own age, Scott Grant.'

'Rat progeny,' Hazel said.

'Ilesy can be quite decent now and then,' Jill replied. 'Well,
by skill and blah he got Scott out of running with a real turdy
gang and after that he didn't pester Hazel no more, although
maybe she liked the pestering.'

'Pus queen,' Hazel said.

'Could *have* met,' Harpur said.

'Yes, could have,' Jill said.

'*Really* turdy,' Harpur said.

'Yes, *really* turdy,' Jill said.

'*Any* more,' Harpur said.

'It was like he gave Scott back to her OK, and he thought it would be crazy after this to do anything that might hurt Scott, such as flashing his vermilion scarf at Haze.' [8]

'As I mentioned, because Mr Iles was so good to us regarding the wall, or at least, half wall, I wanted to make some gesture of repayment,' Doreen Howells said. 'But my husband, Graham, advised not to go to the nick because it would get passed to someone minor on his staff, not to him as an individual, and it was his very individual attention to the broken wall that we wished to reward, not the whole police force as a profession. If at the reception desk I said I wanted to talk to Mr Iles about a wall, or half wall, the officer on duty would not realize the significance, especially if it was only a half wall, and give the matter to some constable. However, we could not find Mr Iles in the telephone book, and my husband said officers with that kind of material for their uniform would be ex-directory. So, if I wanted to persist with it I ought to try for that right-hand man's name instead, being you, if I may say, Mr Harpur, who might pass a message to Mr Iles, or tell us his address.'

'When Mrs Howells says "persist with it" she means not just about a wall,' Jill said. 'This is to do with Mrs Rose Waverton, probably.'

'Pacing about there, obviously intent on something,' Mrs Howells said.

'Mrs Waverton?' Hazel asked.

'That was my impression,' Mrs Howells said, 'confirmed by my hubby.'

'Pacing about to what purpose?' Hazel said. 'Intent on what?'

'I told her she had the spot correct,' Mrs Howells replied. She wore tan corduroy trousers, and a hip-length green top coat over a brown V-necked sweater, no hat, low-heeled brown shoes.

The children had already made tea in the large pot and Hazel went to pour for Harpur. They were using the genuine, thin, china cups. She brought him as well two digestives from the

[8] See *Girls*

biscuit barrel they'd placed on a small table alongside the teapot and Jill's pair of books. Mrs Howells was in a red leather armchair. Harpur took a matching chair opposite. The girls sat each end of a chesterfield, also leather covered, but dark blue.

Mrs Howells said, 'Naturally, this excellent cup of tea puts me in mind of the meeting with . . . no, I was going to say with Mrs Waverton, but I suppose I'd better settle for the lady I *thought* to be Mrs Waverton, and still do. There was a sort of distance to her, a sort of brazen detachment. Graham asked her if she'd like to come into our home for refreshment, actually naming conventional tea, as he phrased it, or iced tea, but she declined. It was as if she had a task, a commitment, and couldn't be bothered with normal politeness.'

'What task?' Jill said.

'You mean looking at the features of the Sandicott–Landau junction, as mentioned at the time of the tragedy in the media?' Hazel said.

'Looking at them features not because she was thinking of another ambush but because she wanted to see whether if someone in the past had come searching for a nice spot for a trap this would do perfect – the buildings, the roads and what-ever,' Jill said.

Harpur decided not to pounce on the bad grammar. His daughter was bravely trying to explain some very complicated strategy, as she saw it, and it would be disrespectful to answer with miserable, measly niggles.

'I'm afraid it annoyed us that she wouldn't accept our invita-tion, just wanted to get on with the job she'd obviously given herself. When she so discourteously rejected our hospitality she said she didn't have time but needed to be "getting along". That was her phrase, "getting along". So casual, so indifferent to our efforts, as though what she would be getting along to was of much higher priority than us. Yet, not everyone would come out on to their lawn and talk to a stranger in helpful fashion, then offer a choice of sup-ups. Her reaction could be seen only as impudent. And the point is, she didn't get along. She stayed asking questions. These were questions that could have been asked in the house while partaking in friendly, responsible style. But, no, she wouldn't allow her snotty self that gracious move. It made the rudeness much, much worse, I think you'll agree. What we felt was we were being used. All this woman was interested in was not us, or our home, but what we might have seen at the junction on a certain date. Her aims were very clear and very specific. They allowed no consideration for others' feelings, such as ours.'

'People can be like that,' Jill said. 'At school we had to consider an ancient, famous remark, "Manners maykth man", with a different spelling from now. It would include women most likely. This is genuine history from a thinker in the church far, far back, but also over the door in a university somewhere even at present.'

'New College, Oxford,' Hazel said.

'But although they maykth man they are often forgot about in this day and age,' Jill said. 'One kid in my class said, "Manners maykth man and man maykth the pigsty."'

'What you're getting at is she might have been trying to guess whether her husband could have come to the junction and recognize it would be great for an attack, like those yobs at the Binnacle suggested,' Hazel said.

'We thought it was something Mr Iles should know about,' Mrs Howells replied. 'We realized it might have a certain bearing on that terrible day the wall got half demolished.'

'Dad sometimes does tell Mr Iles things,' Hazel said.

'We believe very much in manners,' Jill said. 'For instance, we might of told you today, Mrs Howells, that Dad wasn't here and not welcomed you in. But we remembered that saying, "Manners makyth man" (and women and girls in brackets) and we asked you to join us regardless, like, and had tea, biscuits and some charming talks.'

TWENTY-SIX

les said, 'As demanded by that tidy-minded, indefatigably trawling way of mine, Col, I've had some inquiries made into the family of the lad killed at the Binnacle.' Harpur knew that this tidy-minded, indefatigably trawling way of his must have paid off or the assistant chief wouldn't be talking about it now. Those tidy-minded, indefatigably trawling ways of his very often did pay off. If they hadn't, Iles would have discarded those tidy-minded indefatigably trawling ways because they would no longer have been indefatigable. He liked pluses to come from his tidy-minded indefatigably trawling ways.

The ACC had called in at Harpur's headquarters room and was standing at the window gazing fixedly out at the street as if expecting to see sparkling results from his current tidy-minded, indefatigable trawling pretty soon. He wore one of his grey suits, but single-breasted only and unbuttoned. Harpur wondered whether that was to give his body plenty of freedom for the trawling and bringing the catch aboard.

'The dead undergrad, Wyn Normanton Vaughan,' Harpur said. 'Assumed at this stage. We keep an open mind as the formula, non-commital police phrase goes.'

'Yes, assumed and even double assumed at this stage.' Iles paused and glanced back at Harpur over his shoulder. 'But you'll probably ask why I speak of "double", Col.'

'Why do you speak of "double", sir? I don't understand. I meant not officially identified so far. We're still waiting for the parents to get back from Oz.'

'Certainly that's one identification formality we wait for and, in the meantime, we make our assumptions based on information from his friends and the college. But I'm thinking of something shall we say *wider*, Col.'

'Often you're thinking of something wider, sir. I believe it to be part of your tidy-minded, indefatigably trawling nature.

This trawling often takes place in very deep, very extensive waters. Truly wide waters.'

'The inquiries I put in hand began quite satisfactorily,' the ACC said.

'Satisfactorily in which particular, sir?'

'This particular, Harpur: there is, indeed, a family called Vaughan who live where Francis Garland has been told by the university they live. It's in Brecon, Powys, Wales. I wanted to look rather beyond that, though.'

'This is typical of you, sir. Horizons seem to beckon you. Would it be fantasy to say they recognize your noble purpose and count it a privilege to assist?'

'And I got fucking stopped, Harpur.' He whispered this, possibly weakened by the affront he felt. The words, though, bounced back off the window as though fucking stopped themselves, and were completely audible to Harpur; possibly more effectively than if they had come to him direct. This was a message that had met an obstruction – the window – but managed all the same to battle through and get delivered.

'Stopped? Fucking stopped? But how, sir?' Harpur replied. For once it sounded as though a tidy-minded, indefatigable Ilesian trawl had not produced what it should have: very little positive, unless a negative could be regarded as a positive.

'The material dried up,' Iles said.

'Which material?'

'The Vaughan material.'

'Difficult to trace?' Harpur said. 'Some genealogical investigations of this kind can meet formidable snags – documentation missing, or faulty.'

'*Impossible* to trace.'

'But why?'

'It doesn't exist.'

'But Wyn Normanton Vaughan exists, surely, sir, or existed. He was a student of the classics, a bright kid, most probably. He'll be on nominal roles at the university and school. He'll have a stock of special, personal features. For instance, he'd know about that godly shagging swan. Incidentally, sir, I think the myth-maker pinched this tale from that famous old joke.'

'Which famous old joke would that be, then, Harpur?' the ACC asked, his tone radiantly void of interest.

'A god comes down on a forty-eight-hour pass looking for some rumpy-pumpy and afterwards, when he's leaving for heaven, realizes he's been impolite, hasn't introduced himself. "I'm Thor," he says. "Tho am I," the girl replies. "But I'm thatithfied".'

'Did you ever see a film called *The Day Of The Jackal*, Harpur?' Iles replied. 'Detectives trawling through certificates and records to find a name? The task I commissioned is like that, but the opposite. The film detectives thought they'd found what they were after, eventually.'

'Your search didn't come up with what you needed, sir?'

'Blank.'

'Birth, marriage, passport records, property conveyancing?'

'Absent. Null.'

'Were these reliable people doing the search?'

'Entirely. Because I allow you to work with me, Col, you mustn't deduce that I'll make use of any old blunderers.'

'So, how do you react to this impasse, sir?' Harpur replied.

'Oh, there are plenty of Vaughans, of course, plenty of fully authenticated Vaughans.'

'It's a main Welsh surname, with historic overtones, I believe.'

'The *crachach*,' Iles said.

'Sir?'

'Welsh upper-crust. Translates literally as "Nepotism Inc.". The Vaughans get into *The Prime Minister*.'

'"Get into the prime minister", sir? How exactly?'

'In Anthony Trollope's novel, *The Prime Minister*, Col. The Vaughans are mentioned.'

'Oh, yes, absolutely.'

'But I'm looking for Vaughans of a specific Brecon address who tie in with our Wyn Normanton Vaughan – or, at least, the people I briefed for the scour were.'

'And they were the ones who got fucking stopped? They reported back to tell you this, did they, sir?'

'I set up the inquiries, so it's as if I, personally, were fucking stopped by this hiatus, Harpur.'

'I suppose when you go wider there's always a danger of

bumping into an hiatus, sir. Hiatuses flourish in that wider area and can pop up anywhere. My mother used to say, if a hiatus has your name on it you're done for, like with whiz-bang shells in the Great War.'

Iles turned away from the window and sat on the edge of Harpur's desk/work-station. This was a spot he loved: the light from the window fell very sweetly on his fine black lace-ups and his slim legs, not a gross, neon-type glare, but a steady, reverential glow. He said, 'Taking the relevant Vaughan surname, forenames and approximate age we can go back for just over five years and follow the family's activities quite well for that period. The house in Brecon was bought then in the joint names of Gareth Leo Vaughan and Catrin Pamela Vaughan, Wyn Normanton's parents. He joins the local comprehensive school, as does his younger sister, Rhiannon Mary at around that time. Gareth Leo takes a job in local government. These details are easy to come by and stand consistent with one another.

'But what we don't have, Col, is anything on the family *before* this. No, as it were, pre-context. Why I say "blank". Why I say "absent". We don't know and can't discover, where they lived before Brecon. We don't know and can't discover where the children previously went to school. We don't know and can't discover where the father worked, or, if he didn't work, where he drew welfare. We don't know and can't discover whether this was a first marriage for either Gareth Leo or Catrin Pamela. In fact, we don't know and can't discover whether they are married to each other at all or just partners.

'Wyn Normanton Vaughan qualifies for university under that name because this falls within the five-year period available to us. His second forename might seem to have a geographical significance but we've gone through school records, register of electors, hospital records, job centre records, dole records in Normanton, West Yorkshire, near Wakefield, but blank, absent. It's possible that the name, Normanton, has been deliberately given as a false lead.'

'Given who by?' Harpur said.

'So what do you make of it, Col?' Iles replied.

Harpur saw, of course, that there was only one thing to make of it. The blankness, the absences, were resoundingly communicative: no need for an interpreter. But the ACC liked to handle revelations, disclosures, deductions himself, for the amazement and slavering admiration of Harpur. And, because Harpur frequently held back crucial items of information from the assistant chief, it seemed reasonable and decent to balance matters by playing Dumbo to him now and then; and to do a wholehearted gasp or two of astonishment at his brain-power bordering on wizardry.

'A veritable puzzler, sir,' Harpur said weakly. 'Were they non-persons until Brecon?'

'In France, Harpur, some immigrant groups refer to themselves as "les sans papiers" – people with no official documentation because they came into the country illegally, and therefore without identity.'

'The Vaughans are almost like this except there *is* documentation for them during the last five years – just as there would be documentation of the immigrants back in their own country.'

'Sounds impossible, sir.' It didn't but Harpur would humour Iles. The ACC loved to be thought of as Mr Know-All. It could be considered cruel to let him discover that what Mr Know-All knew was also known by at least one other. Iles's ego had to be sensitively catered for.

The assistant chief gave him an exceptionally kind, patient smile, like a teacher trying to encourage a thicko with his two-times table. The ACC obviously decided to offer Harpur a clue. 'Think back to the Templedon family, Col.'

'The Templedons?'

'What did I do . . . we do there? Can you recall?'

'You – we – moved the family into a safe house on our ground because they were in very considerable danger elsewhere.[9] Robert Templedon had been a super-grass in another part of GB and needed to disappear. The relatives and associates of those super-grassed and jailed are likely to want vengeance.'

'Correct, Harpur! Brilliantly done. But what else?'

'You – we – arranged new employment, new schools and so on for them.'

[9] See *Wolves of Memory*

'Once more incontestably accurate, Col. But what else?'

'There's even more?'

'Think. Focus on something absolutely basic.'

'Basic?'

'Shall I say the word "names", to you?' Iles replied gently, extending the charitable leg-up of the clue.

'Oh, yes, of course, of course,' Harpur cried delightedly but apologetically for having been so slow. 'You – we – gave them changed names. They had been, what was it . . . yes, they had been Ballions, hadn't they, but became Templedons?'

'And they are happy and unhurt, successfully hidden away as Templedons on our ground even now, aren't they, Col?'

'Adaptability. Guided adaptability by you . . . us.'

'And what did that new family name require?'

'Require, sir?'

'What must the re-start names have, Col, something indispensable?'

'Well, clearly, acceptance by the families.'

Iles nodded impatiently as though Harpur's answer went without saying. 'Yes, fair enough, acceptance. As you imply, that's obvious. But what more? What is vital?'

'It shouldn't be an awkward new name. There was that actress, Diana Dors, whose real name was Fluck. A name like that would leave them open to rough jokes and deliberate errors with the "l" left out. I suppose Dors could be mistakenly spoken as drawers but that's nothing like as rude.'

'OK, not Fluck. Not Dors. Not Tosser. But yet one further essential,' Iles said.

Harpur thought the game could be brought to an end now. 'Ah!' he said with terrific warmth, as though suddenly hit by wonderful inspiration of epiphany grade. 'Ah!'

'You've got it, have you, Col?'

'Ah! Obliteration.'

'So true, Harpur.'

'Elimination totally of their previous name, Balllion, their previous identities, their family history. A sort of imposed amnesia or they might be traced, Ballion equals Templedon.'

'As with?'

'As with the Vaughans,' Harpur replied, 'and whatever their

name and location were before that. Isn't there a Home Office department whose only function is to wipe out all previous bureaucratic and other traces of an ex-informant and his family when they secretly take on a new life?'

'I knew you'd see it eventually, Col. The "sans papiers" in France are sans papiers because they are sans papiers – without papers. But the Vaughans, or whatever their name was before, did have all the proper papers in that earlier name, and these papers, and all other traces, had to be removed in order to put an unbridgeable distance between their past identities and their new ones. That's why your term, Col, "obliteration" was so brilliantly appropriate.'

'Thank you, sir.'

'This is an obliteration, not of the people themselves, obviously, but of their history – of their entire history up until that point five years ago when their new life begins.'

'So we think Gareth Leo Vaughan has form, do we?' Harpur said.

'He'll be some kind of villain, ex-villain, turned former major confidential source, most probably, and the powers must have decided to lose him and his in mid-Wales – no other force to be informed, for fear of leaks. They've been given Welsh first names, neutral second forenames, or faux-geographical. Nothing over the top. It's been a subtle operation. Tricky, but perhaps others beside myself could have unscrambled it.'

'That I doubt, sir,' Harpur said. 'How does all this affect the present Wyn Normanton Vaughan's death and general situation?'

'You're looking for links, aren't you, Col, not just to Wyn Normanton Vaughan but to Frank Waverton, who was adjacent to the Binnacle incident, at least adjacent.'

'Certainly.'

'I thought you would be, Col.'

'Yes?'

'Oh, yes.'

'And?'

'Oh, yes, I knew it. With you there comes a point where your intelligence will kick in. The process is fascinating to observe but the lengthy wait can become very depressing.'

'I'm sorry, sir.'

TWENTY-SEVEN

G enerally, Iles was OK in morgues. He might be totally restrained and unthespian, no violence or cursing, a decent decorousness. The dead couldn't fuck him up and so he respected them heartily, above all savouring their silence. He felt able to lay his paranoia restfully alongside one of them for a while. Also, Iles was very keen on cleanliness and mortuaries usually looked spruce.

At funerals he could turn less manageable. They had a theatrical element, anyway, even before some dramatic, play-within-a-play, rumbustious performance by Iles. Occasionally, he seemed forced by inner urges to take a semi-starring role and offer one of his rasping soliloquies about knitting as a pastime for the elderly, or social decline, or malice directed at him personally by a named mandarin, or named mandarins, at the Home Office.

He would denounce a congregation for not backing him in these disputes and if Harpur managed to whisper to him that the congregation would not have heard of the injustices until he mentioned them now, Iles would reply that to him it looked like a congregation who, if they *had* been aware of this suffering, they would have passed by on the other side, a Biblical phrase sent to condemn religious do-nothing arseholes.

The Wyn Normanton Vaughan funeral would be in Wales. Iles might decide to go. It depended on his mood that day. Or he might send Chief Inspector Francis Garland, who had the case. It was the kind of tragic death where a senior police officer should be present to represent the law-abiding community's regret and official sympathy. If Iles did go, Harpur would have to accompany him in case the ACC turned showy, loud, and tumultuous, as though he'd forgotten the serious reason for his attendance.

At funerals, Harpur had to be ready to suppress physically all flagrantly off-colour behaviour by the ACC. This could be massively difficult. Harpur invariably wore at least a jock-strap and preferably a groin-protecting cricket box when attending a funeral with Iles. It amused Harpur in an uncomfortable sort of way that while the majority of people attending a funeral thought most about the kind of dark clothes they should wear, he had to be primarily concerned that his balls didn't get pulverized, while in the background, the organist might be doing a solemn anthem. Harpur would also take a knuckle-duster in his pocket if during the day or two before the funeral Iles seemed especially on edge. Iles merely on edge was worrying enough but *exceptionally* on edge hinted at a likely shit-storm.

The assistant chief might not be heavily made but he possessed fierce, wiry strength and a good knowledge of the body's weaker areas. Also, Harpur thought he must have been on a long, very thorough course in advanced head-butting at one of the training centres for staff rank officers.

Now and then, he would attempt to take absolute command of a funeral service and could grow violent towards the priest, vicar, minister or members of the congregation if they resisted and tried to keep him out of the pulpit; and many would see it as a holy duty to keep him out of the pulpit. Harpur hated fighting on pulpit steps because if Iles had already nearly reached the top when Harpur intervened, the ACC would have the option of kicking down vehemently with one of his lace-up, custom-made black shoes and catching him in the face. Iles had played rugby to quite a high level and still refereed now and then. He knew what a tactical kicking could do to cheekbones, teeth and chin. Obvious wounds and bruises of that kind seemed to Harpur not proper at a solemn religious gig. A place of worship should not be turned into a first-aid centre.

Although the ACC had carefully chosen black shoes to suit the mourning nature of the occasion, Harpur considered it grotesquely *infra dig* to have one toe cap bright with blood, particularly his.

Incense always got up the assistant chief's nose and he would become especially hunnish in any church where it was flung about backed by chanting. 'Take that fucking fly-spray away you festooned, robed jerk,' he'd yelled at a high-Anglican funeral last year. Iles was brought up super-Prot in Northern Ireland and despised what he called 'fancy sacerdotal glad-rags'.

He and Harpur went to the mortuary with Wyn Normanton's parents and Francis Garland. Iles and Garland were in uniform, Harpur had on a dark suit and unflashy tie. As they entered the hospital, Iles said to Wyn Normanton's mother, 'One identification will be quite adequate. If you would prefer to wait in the foyer we'll rejoin you very shortly.'

'I've flown back from Adelaide to get here today. I want to see him.'

'Forgive me. I understand,' Iles replied. 'Certainly I understand.'

'Thanks, then.' She sounded surprised at the ACC's kindness. To an extent, it had shocked Harpur, also. Harpur knew him, though, and was bound to find any sign of consideration for others' feelings from Iles disorientating. They did show now and then, and always caught Harpur unprepared. But, on the other hand, these were the first moments Mrs Vaughan had ever met the ACC. Her reaction must mean she usually regarded the police – all police, not just Iles – as the enemy. This might fit the guess by the assistant chief and Harpur himself that the Vaughans had something dubious, something crooked, in their past. They might have moved out of that category now, but ancient attitudes possibly lingered.

Catrin Pamela Vaughan would be in her early forties, he thought, about 5' 5", still wearing the lightweight slacks and top she'd presumably taken to Australia. Her hair was in a fringe with the rest straight down to her shoulders on each side. It had been given a very black dye job. She had kept herself slim and almost thin. She had small features and an attractive oval face which, combined with the hairstyle, put him in mind of Liz Taylor as Cleopatra on one of the movie channels.

At the trolley she and her husband stood close to the covered body, the back of their hands possibly touching; not holding hands, but perhaps a contact, maybe some mutual comfort and support getting transferred. Harpur and Iles stood behind them. When an attendant pulled back the sheet covering Wyn Normanton Vaughan, she stared for a couple of seconds, then said, 'Yep,' and turned away, as if prepared to leave. She'd come all that distance to see him, and now she *had* seen him and that was it, thanks very much. The attendant drew the sheet into place, then took them to a small side room.

This was an established procedure. Harpur had seen it on previous cases. Visitors were given the chance to recover before going back to life outside. The room had a drinking-water dispenser and a stack of plastic cups. Iles filled a cup for her and then one for all the others and himself. There was paperwork to be completed and the attendant left them while he saw to that. He'd return for a signature or signatures on the identification certificate.

Iles said to the couple, 'You'll go home now?'

'Well, we're not flying back to Adelaide,' Mrs Vaughan said. 'Our daughter was staying with friends while we were away. We'll pick her up en route.'

'Brecon, isn't it?' Iles said. 'A lovely town. The cathedral and castle. Salman Rushdie hid out there at the beginning of the fatwa, I believe. But that would be before your time, I expect.'

Iles waited for a second, obviously inviting the Vaughans to do a bit of dating for him. They stayed quiet, though, sipping the water.

'Language,' Iles said.

'Language?' she said.

'Welsh. Any problems?' Iles replied. 'Rushdie's wife at the time wrote afterwards that they'd been through Brecon and Aberhonddu, not realizing they were the same place.'

'Plenty of English spoken there,' Catrin said.

'So you're well settled in?' Iles said.

'Yes, it's a fine town,' Gareth Leo replied.

'I notice neither of you has picked up a Welsh accent yet,' Iles replied.

'Takes time, I expect,' Gareth Leo said.

'You've had only five years, I think,' Iles said.

'Right,' Vaughan said.

'Your accents?' Iles said. 'I'd say south-east England, possibly London, previously. It would take some adjusting to a rural spot like Brecon.'

'Slowly does it,' she said.

'Yes, south-east England or London itself,' Iles said. 'Accents

interest me. I wouldn't put myself on a par with the prof in
My Fair Lady, but I'm improving. I'd diagnose both of you as
south of the Thames, Lewisham, Penge, that way? It's own
brand of cockney. Some very good schools around those parts,
I understand.'

Harpur thought it might be gangland, too. He could see that
neither of the Vaughans felt sure how to deal with Iles. If it
was fact that they had been shipped off to a safe house in Wales
five years or so ago, they might not realize that the secrecy of
the move would be absolute – no general notification to all
police forces. One force, the host, would have to be told and
only top people there. Nobody else. The Vaughans might
think Iles was merely toying with them for his own purposes,
already knew all the answers to his questions. In some ways
they would be right, Harpur decided. Iles had cracked the
security barrier.

'And talking of schools, the one at Brecon must have some
top-rate teachers,' Iles said. 'Wyn Normanton would need very
good grades to get into university here. It's not Oxford or
Cambridge, admittedly, but is well regarded, entry requirements
high. Perhaps, though, it's unfair to give all the credit to the
Brecon sixth form. He must already have had a very sound
earlier education.'

Again Iles waited for some confirming detail. This time
Gareth Leo did respond. But he must have had practice in
some of that blankness the ACC encountered during his
researches. 'Oh, yes,' Vaughan said. Nothing more. He'd be
about the same age as Catrin, very solidly made, just under six
feet tall, maybe puzzled by Iles's persistent fishing about his
and the family's past, but strong enough in the head, and determined enough, to block inconvenient questions. Harpur could
imagine him doing the same under formal police interrogation.
Did Vaughan have experience of that, though not as Gareth Leo
Vaughan? Perhaps he had resisted so well at one of those
sessions – the last, most likely – as his way to a bargaining
situation: a new, hideaway life for him and his family in return
for the kind of information his interrogators wanted.

His fair hair was in what could be fast retreat but the remainder
he kept long and brushed back hard in thick swathes over his

ears. He wore a cream-coloured, two-piece summer suit and
white, open-necked shirt. They looked fine, despite the long
flight. Maybe he'd had time to change. He had what Harpur's
mother would have called an 'aristocratic face', meaning a
mildly ridged, Roman nose. His jaw was slabby, his blue eyes
defiant and wily and, of course, sad now.

Harpur could imagine him as part of a crooked outfit – drugs,
and/or protection, and/or top class robbery somewhere around
those south London districts named by Iles; but could imagine
him also realizing that this time the case, cases, against him
looked too much to get away with and therefore willing to do
a super-grass deal. There was a famous, popular Welsh song
that went something like: 'We'll keep a welcome in the hillside,
we'll keep a welcome in the vales'. Vaughan, or whatever he
was called then, might have been ready to accept that welcome
and move away to Brecon.

'As we understand from the media, Wyn got into some kind
of disturbance at a late-night hotel do, but it seemed to have
been calmed down by a pusher there,' Vaughan said.

'A Frank Waverton,' she said.

'Yes,' Garland said, 'that's how it seems to have started –
some alleged trouble about a girl. We had trouble tracing her.
She tells us the incident was very badly misinterpreted.'

'So who is he?' Vaughan said.

'Waverton? He operates in one of the city's bigger businesses,'
Garland said. 'Married, thirties, keeps trim hill jogging near their
house in Viaduct Avenue, the old Heritage viaduct site, new
Merc, smart dresser, no off-the-peg, daughter, Olive, at a comp,
good swimmer.'

'What kind of business?' she asked.

Iles said, 'We have a policy of toleration here.'

'A drugs firm?' Vaughan asked.

Harpur could sense him focusing very hard on Waverton.
Crooks, ex-crooks could be like that. They needed an objective,
one objective only, and they put all their attention on it. 'He
has a middle-management role,' Harpur said.

'And from the reports we gather he had something . . . well,
something sort of shameful in his past,' Catrin said.

Harpur found it odd to hear her talk like that when Iles had just been trying to discover whether they had something shameful in *their* past, when they were not called Vaughan. It continued to amaze him how apparently very separate events and situations suddenly became linked with other very separate events and situations.

'Could Wyn have been caught up in some sort of turf war?' Vaughan asked. 'Had he become a user?'

'I've explained, we don't have turf wars,' Iles said. 'Tolerance.'

'But you do have fatal knifings,' Catrin said.

'This guy, Waverton, is obviously at the hotel do to sell stuff,' Vaughan said. Harpur thought he sounded familiar with that kind of commerce. 'There's a fracas. He comes over immediately and gets involved.'

'Not really involved,' Garland said. 'Our information is that he tried to quell the trouble then withdrew.'

'Your information might not be complete, though, might it?'

'In which aspect?' Iles said.

'The squabble – it could have been about a girl. It could have been about something else,' Vaughan said. 'This kind of rave, there can be all kinds of aggro and threats.' Once more he spoke like someone who had often seen such tensions and hates. 'Maybe this guy knew Waverton, had some kind of business connection with him.'

'Which guy?' Harpur said.

'The one who did Wyn, of course,' Catrin Vaughan said.

'You two have obviously discussed the accounts of the tragedy, and that's only natural,' Iles said. 'But you mustn't take speculation as fact.'

'The *fact* is that when Waverton goes, as you think, to restore a bit of order he's dealing with what seems to be a simple punch-up – fists and shoving, nothing worse. It happens all the time at raves,' Vaughan said. 'He leaves them and suddenly we find one of the crowd now has a knife.' He lowered his head. Then he added, matter-of-factly, almost: 'And he uses it on Wyn,' like polishing off an equation.

Iles gave one of his grunts. It could be surprise. It could signal he'd been granted a revelation.

'What are you saying?' Garland asked. 'That Waverton on the quiet passed the knife to the assailant. We've nothing at all to that effect. He has been interviewed but only as a witness.'

'He's not going to tell you he provided a mate with a knife that's going to kill someone only minutes later, is he?' Catrin replied.

'Mr Iles, you say there are no turf wars here, and you might believe it,' Vaughan said, 'but where there are drugs there is envy and suspicion and jockeying and attempts to colonize. The girl might have next to nothing to do with this.'

'You know about these things?' Iles said.

'Perhaps you think if you don't have any outright battles, any blood on the pavement, your tolerance policy is working fine,' Vaughan said. 'The violence and jostling for control can still go on out of sight, though. There's a lad under a sheet in that other room to prove it, wounds tactfully patched.'

'Yes, the girl contacted us, very distressed at having, as she put it, "caused the death",' Garland said. 'She's eighteen, a literature undergraduate. She had come to the party with the man we're holding. But in one of the band's rest spells she'd heard your lad, Wyn, talking to someone else and thought she recognized his accent – south London, Lewisham way? She comes from that area herself. She wanted to swap stuff with him about streets and shops and schools, the way people do when away from home.

'But the music started banging again and it became crazy to be discussing fine points about accents, so they went for a few minutes into the toilets – what she called "the stinking Augean toilets" – but he told her he wasn't from her part of the world at all. "Brecon", he said. She couldn't believe it, kept on at him, but he stuck to that –"Brecon".'

'Well, of course he would,' Gareth Leo Vaughan said. 'She'd got that very wrong, hadn't she?'

'Obviously,' Iles said, 'she must have imagined the resemblance.'

'But the boyfriend misread the absence,' Garland said. 'He thought an assignation, a betrayal, so he starts the trouble. That's how it looks. We're at the alleged state only so far, of course.'

'And then comes that other misunderstanding, does it?' Vaughan said. 'Waverton thinks it's a drugs dispute and comes over and passes the knife to someone who presumably had a dealing connection with him.'

'We don't know that,' Garland said. 'And, clearly, the girl said nothing along those lines. Just confusion over the accents.'

The mortuary man came back and approached Vaughan with identification statements to be signed. 'Catrin can do it,' he said. To Harpur it sounded as though Vaughan himself didn't want closure yet, and completing the papers might be mistaken for that.

The Vaughans left. They'd come in their car parked long-term at Heathrow while they were in Australia. Iles, Harpur and Francis Garland went back to police headquarters and Iles came to Harpur's room again. He wanted to see the witness statement taken by a detective sergeant from Waverton.

Harpur screened it. He'd read the statement before and considered there was not much more there than had appeared in the media. Waverton told the sergeant that he was at the Binnacle that night and at one point had noticed some kind of altercation among a group of young men and women. He'd regarded this as nothing unusual at raves but kept an eye. It had seemed to get worse, out of control. He'd feared that this would break out into serious violence and had crossed the dance floor to try to 'nip the quarrel in the bud'. He said he'd felt a duty, being older than these kids, more responsible.

And he thought he had quietened things and returned to his original spot near the main doors. The sergeant hadn't pressed for an explanation of why he was at the hotel. Waverton was adult, entitled to stay up late and go where he wished. He lived in a tolerant realm. True, the rave might be illegal and involve trespass, but Waverton hadn't organized it.

In his statement Waverton said that to his astonishment when he looked back towards the group he'd recently been talking to the fighting had begun again and he saw one of the young men fall and not get up. Waverton said he thought the man might have been struck with an object, not by a punch. The fighting stopped, as though people had come to realize something serious had happened. Several of the group seemed to get down and try to give first aid, possibly with kiss of life. Waverton didn't feel he could help any further and hadn't intervened again.

The sergeant asked whether Waverton had heard any shouting,

possibly referring to him and in an unfavourable tone. 'There might have been shouting,' Waverton replied, 'but not audible from where I was, because the music continued to drown out any other sound for at least another couple of minutes. I couldn't say whether there were remarks about me. I suppose some of the group thought I had no business intruding on them.'

'That was the gist of the shouting we're told, but more particular, more specific, than because of simple annoyance at getting told off by you,' the sergeant said.

'No, can't help you on that,' Waverton replied.

Harpur saw deep frustration in Iles. He was sitting on an ordinary straight-backed wooden chair, not in his usual spot on Harpur's desk. He crouched forward, staring at the screen even when the statement had finished. More of that blankness he seemed dogged by had moved in on him. Sight of his legs and shoes could no longer bring balm.

Harpur tried to guess at the ACC's thinking now. He seemed conscious of a gravely dire network of troubles, none of which he could annihilate. There was this slippery figure, Waverton, perhaps as elegantly clothed as Iles himself, and fine shoes, stepping into prominence, possibly even showing some public spirit; and yet Iles would still want to know whether he set up the Sandicott murders.

And then came the Vaughans with their closed-off, expertly expunged background and possible infinitely awful link to Waverton. Iles, unrelaxed, miserable, multi-thwarted on that basic piece of furniture looked as though he knew defeat, and could not see how to recover from it. He must fear that management of the situation, the situations, was slipping away from him; or had already slipped away from him. That notion would mash his ego. That notion would delight his enemies. 'I think I'll have to talk to Waverton myself, Harpur.'

This might be a sign of the turmoil he was suffering: assistant chiefs didn't normally interview witnesses, especially when one of his officers had already done that job.

'The sergeant questioned Waverton well enough, but he didn't have the full picture, did he? How could he?' Iles said.

'What *is* the full picture, sir?' Harpur asked.

'Quite, Col,' Iles replied.

TWENTY-EIGHT

Ralph Ember liked to be at the club he owned in Shield Terrace a little while before it opened at lunchtime and then again late at night and into the small hours when it was busiest. He went through something of a ritual at close-down of the Monty. First, he'd bag the day's takings for dropping off in the bank's wall safe on the way home. Then he'd do a careful check around the outside of the building for possible delayed action fire bombs left by business rivals and/or folk he'd crossed, though he tried unflinchingly to abide by a rule he'd made for himself, namely, not to shag any member's wife or girlfriend, no matter how persuasively some women came on to him. Those who brushed their hand across his trousers in the groin area probably imagined they were giving him a treat and a taster whereas Ralph found such behaviour totally out of harmony with the elite character he sought for the club. Ralph thought that in the Monty the word 'member' should have only the one, obvious meaning, a paid-up customer of the club.

The afternoons he tried to reserve for a sleep and general relaxation at Low Pastures, his manor house on a hillock over-looking the city. He had taken up archery not long ago and was practising today in one of the paddocks after his nap. The children were at their private school and Ralph's wife, Margaret, had gone to her regular watercolour class. Ralph approved of this as a hobby for her and, although he didn't think much of the stuff she did, he insisted on having some of the pictures framed and hung in the hall of Low Pastures, properly lit. He considered it would be rude and very hurtful to let her see his real opinion. Elsewhere in the house he had some genuine art on the walls, several of the works quite possibly valuable and not fakes.

The afternoon weather was excellent for archery, a helpful breeze coming from behind him and good visibility for the divisions of the target. It greatly pleased Ralph to feel he was in touch with history through his bow and arrows. Of course, he had a fairly frequent reminder of that history when at one of those combined company dinners in the Agincourt. Victory over the French so many years ago was commemorated in that name, and had been secured by skilled use of the longbow, despite our side being outnumbered.

Ralph couldn't remember ever reading whether those British archers had the luck of the wind helping their arrows along, but he felt certain they'd have done OK anyway. He thought that as he improved he would set up a practising session when the wind came head-on and powerful. This would help put him in better touch with those old valiant and skillful warriors. He tried never to molly-coddle himself. If there was a similarity between him and Henry V's troops, Ralph wanted it to be authentic. He felt very certain that suppose he'd been alive in those days he would have been one of Henry's troops, possibly with an officer rank.

He was walking forward to recover a batch of arrows in or near the target when he heard someone call his name. Actually, he realized he'd automatically fallen into a military style of moving as he thought of the battle, and it was more like a brisk march as he went to collect the arrows.

He turned and saw Manse Shale pushing a mountain bike. On his visit to the rectory, Ralph had noticed several bicycles, including an ancient Humber with chain guard that he used around the town. He had on a helmet, black, below-the-knee Lycra shorts, and a striped green and beige sports shirt. 'Just out for a country trundle, Ralph, and suddenly realized I was passing the barns of Apsley Farm and therefore must be very near your place. Thought I'd chance it and look in,' Shale said.

Manse was clearly trying to make it sound casual, an accident. Ralph reckoned it must have been carefully planned, though, Shale probably knew he'd be home most afternoons. Manse might want a confidential chat and feel the Monty was too crowded and obvious. But he would also know that Ralph did everything he could to keep his home and family entirely separate from his business life. So, Manse would sneak in like this, pretend it was an offshoot of a Lycra spin.

It infuriated Ralph to hear Shale speak of 'your place', meaning Low Pastures, as if it was some council flat or dismal semi. And he resented hearing Apsley Farm described as being 'very near' Low Pastures. Not even remotely true: Low Pastures stood very much alone, with excellent views in all directions, and not hemmed in by any other workaday buildings, such as Apsley's barns. Shale's absurd comments were clearly his attempt to downgrade Ralph's property and estate, turn it into the sort of ordinary residence someone taking a bike ride might feel like dropping in on, offering no forewarning, and certainly without an invitation.

Here he was in that fucking ridiculous gear, obviously intending to discuss Waverton and his removal. He couldn't risk possible phone taps, or a conversation at the club. His hamster face, but with ferrety eyes, resembled a hamster's even more strongly under his gaudy crimson and blue helmet. Ralph couldn't understand why that was the case. After all, a cycling helmet had no hamster qualities. But that's how it was for Ralph. Manse should be in one of those two-tier cages, not trying to bike his way into a distinguished country house. To come out here on a bike, and in that farcical outfit, to discuss an impending death seemed to Ralph a total disregard for tone. Surely some respect should be shown towards the prospective corpse.

But, unavoidably, Ralph had to ask him in. Ember loathed discourtesy. Manse left his bike leaning against the target, which to Ember seemed another foul breach of decorum. Ralph couldn't escape the impression that it ruptured the brilliant resemblance between his new sport and the grand conquerors at Agincourt many centuries ago. He felt that there was something plebeian and disorganized about a bike left leaning against anything, let alone an archery target with such glorious historic overtones.

As they walked to the house Manse said in his special kind of English, 'On the gate to the grounds I seen a plaque with what seems to me like outright Latin, Ralph.'

'It's outside and you're right, it's Latin, so I suppose you could call it outright, Manse. Low Pastures had a lord lieutenant living here at one stage, and at a different time, the Spanish consul. These would be educated people. One of them probably had the plaque installed. The gate itself has been renewed more than once, I imagine, but the plaque has survived. I feel it a duty to preserve it – make sure the screws don't rust allowing the plaque to fall and possibly get trampled and broken.'

'Of course, Caring had Low Pastures for a while, didn't he, Ralph?' Shale said. 'But I wouldn't think he put no Latin plaque there.'

This was another dirty gambit from him. 'I believe the plaque would have been there long before Caring,' Ember said at once and in a very definite voice. A villain called Oliver Leach, known as Caring, because of his constant worried look, did live in Low Pastures at one time. Shale wanted to hint there was a rubbishy side to the house as well as a Spanish consul. Caring and Peter Chitty, both dead now, had been a middling successful robber team. 'The Latin means: "A man's mind is what he is",' Ralph replied. 'Or "The mind of each man is the man himself." Cicero.'

'He did quite a lot of sayings, I believe,' Manse said.

'Yes, quite a lot.'

'He knew how to put his finger on a great truth and write it nice and short. Them days, before TV or the World Cup, people had a lot of time for thinking about things and getting their ideas down on papyrus, as jotters were called then, unless they was galley slaves,' Shale said. 'It would be hard to argue against them remarks about a man's mind.'

'Yes, Cicero could be pretty sharp, I gather,' Ralph said.

'If a man didn't have a mind he wouldn't know he didn't have a mind because he wouldn't have anything to know it with. This would leave him in quite a situation,' Manse said.

Ember saw that the blather was meant to slow things down a little so the real reason for the Manse visit could be gently eased into the conversation later, not hurled at Ralph immediately, perhaps annoying him, perhaps even offending so much by the bluntness that he would reject any further Waverton discussion. Shale was what was called in some occupations 'a progress chaser'. That is, someone sent to speed up work on some job. Manse had sent himself. The job was Waverton. The worker was Ralph, or should be.

Ralph took him into the house. Ember wondered whether

this property had ever seen anything like Shale in his pedal-power outfit. Perhaps there had been fancy dress parties, popular among the landed gentry in the Victorian period. Or the Spanish consul might have liked get-togethers with a theme from his own country and asked people to come as matadors or flamenco dancers. But Low Pastures would be more used to people clothed formally for business or ceremonial occasions in the city, or booted and spurred after hunting. Manse had at least taken the helmet off as a gesture of respect.

They went into what Ralph referred to as the Round Room, because of its curved walls, with a huge window at one end giving a view of the distant sea. The room had a four-leaf mahogany table, big Edwardian armchairs, the frames re-covered in moquette, a chesterfield, also moquetted, and a mahogany chiffonier.

'I won't offer you a Kressmann Armagnac, Manse,' Ember said, 'it might affect your balance on the bike, but I've got some tomato juice.' He brought a bottle from the chiffonier and a couple of glasses. Ralph poured for both of them.

Manse gazed at the art around the walls. 'I'm a pre-Raphaelite man myself, as you probably know, Ralph. Dante Gabriel Rossetti I can't get enough of, not to mention Burne-Jones. Brotherhood. They had a brotherhood. I love that idea. Say one of them runs out of blue – they done a lot of blue for women's dresses – yes, if DG was out of blue one of the others would get around to the Arts and Crafts shop and bring a couple of tubes of blue for his mate, like "Compliments of the Brotherhood".' He took a long pull at the juice. 'Waverton, Ralph,' he said.

Out it came at last, the real reason for this wonderfully casual call! The obviousness of the scheming was so strong Ralph almost laughed. 'Waverton?' he replied.

'Still with us,' Shale said.

'Certain unexpected developments brought delays and some confusion, Manse, although they seemed to have no basic connection with our project. There's a philosophy about this kind of random snag and the need for us all to fight back and do our own thing, regardless.'

'Is this Cicero?'

'Later. Existentialism.'

'Are we still as we were, Ralph – a brotherhood ready to aid each other in a major matter?' Shale replied.

Ralph didn't fancy being brother to this freakish looking hamster clone, but he said, 'Why shouldn't we be still as we were, Manse? There might be blips in our approach, but blips are only blips, and can be by-passed, can be removed.'

Shale gave a great beam of a smile that to quite a degree humanized his face. This transformation shook Ember, its force, its scale. His teeth were full-sized, not hamster teeth. 'I knew – knew – you'd stand by me, Ralph. And I know – know – that when the time comes I'll stand by you after the same honourable fashion.'

'The problem hasn't shifted, Manse,' Ralph declared. 'There still has to be recompense for the murder of your wife and son. Matters have to proceed as you and I want. The future for our two firms requires this.'

And Ralph meant it. Even apart from the existentialist compulsion, it would be unthinkable, surely, to show himself scared or indecisive in front of this farcical two-wheel-fan. The point was, Ralph didn't in the least consider he had been cowardly to dodge out at the Binnacle crisis when he saw all the police and ambulance activity. To withdraw had been wise, in fact, tactically brilliant. That did not amount to panic. But he considered it would be panicky now to make that incident a warning and discard any notion of seeing to Waverton. Ralph valued the soldierly comradeship he'd felt lately with those longbow lads at Agincourt. They hadn't chickened because there were so few of them against so many.

And Ralph must not chicken because of an inconvenient, irrelevant event at a rave. Just before the Binnacle hadn't he reached a solid decision to do Waverton as per agreement with Shale? Up until then, he had felt very uncertain. To scamper back to that uncertainty now, or even worse than uncertainty, would be pathetic, a ghastly endorsement of those vicious labels, Panicking Ralph or Panicking Ralphy.

Shale stood and put on his helmet. 'Do you know, I got to admit I'd sort of given up believing you'd do it, Ralph. In fact, I thought of going down to the Binnacle that night because I'd heard he'd be there. Do it myself. In the crowd they get at them music nights I thought I might be able to slink in, then slink out when the attack was finished. But, of course, the spot became full of police and whatall, so I had to chuck it and get clear.'

Ralph smiled. 'You actually went there, did you? You must have missed half a night's sleep.'

They walked back to Manse's bike at the target. Shale said, 'Did you ever think of calling yourself Rafe not Ralph as some do, Ralph, especially upper-class people in the Household Cavalry and that sort of gang because – no offence – to ralph in America means to throw-up. The same sort of sound, what's termed "echoic", my daughter told me. So, someone might say, "I'm feeling a bit echoic. I think I'm going to ralph."'

TWENTY-NINE

'I don't know how you'll view this, sir,' Harpur said.

'In which particular, Col?' Iles said.

'You come at things in a very . . . a very *individual* way occasionally. I've heard folk say after meeting you for the first time, "That's an individual if I ever encountered one."'

'Are you saying in your usual slippery, bet-hedged way that I'm fucking insane, Harpur?'

'What I have to ask myself, sir, is whether what we have here is a plus or a minus, a plus or minus as far as it concerns your quest,' Harpur replied. 'It's as if in one respect your quest has been satisfactorily concluded, though without your direct participation. And yet, in another respect it means your quest can never be concluded in the fullest sense of that term.'

'Which?'

'Which what, sir?'

'Term.'

'Concluded.'

'Has his wife been told?' Iles replied.

'Garland sent Sergeant Pate and a couple of WPCs, one WPC to stay with their daughter, if necessary.'

Harpur and Iles were on a hillside overlooking the city, not far from the remnants of the old viaduct, and not far, either, from the concrete anti-aircraft gun emplacements used in the war, another spot where Harpur sometimes rendezvoused in secret with his main and supreme informant, Jack Lamb.

It wasn't Lamb who had phoned Harpur a couple of hours ago, though, but the headquarters Control Room again. An inspector there said they'd had a frightened, only half-coherent call about the find from a pair of lads who'd been out after rabbits on Torson Steep at first light. Chief Inspector Garland had also been informed. 'The ACC will want to know at once, too,' Harpur had said.

'Right, sir.'

Denise, wearing a black, sleeveless vest she'd found in one
of the bedroom chest drawers, and asleep alongside Harpur had
snorted and whimpered at the interruption but didn't properly
wake up. Her sleeps usually took her ten fathoms deep where,
she'd told Harpur, all her dreams were tinted indigo. She'd
automatically pushed a hand towards the ciggies on the bedside
table, two of them left ready, part out of the packet, but full
unconsciousness got her again and stopped that. Her hand fell
helplessly on to the duvet like a shot bird. Her fingers twitched
as if they knew they'd been cast aside from their life work and
furiously resented it.

The inspector on the Control Room phone could and would
make what he wanted of the background accompaniment to his
conversation with Harpur. He reckoned he must have heard the
bell more or less at once this time. Hazel and Jill hadn't left
their beds to quiz him on the reason for going out so damn
early, possibly disrupting breakfast.

On Torson Steep now, Iles said, 'I think I catch your drift,
Col.'

'As to which particular, sir?'

'As to how to regard this, one way or its very reverse.'

'Tricky. I thought you might see what we have here as a kind
of rough justice.'

Iles pondered this for a second and then said, 'I'm certainly
in favour of that occasionally, or oftener.' He was in civvies
this morning, a long, admiral-of-the-fleet style ankle-length grey
top-coat, a dark red woollen bobble hat, a vermilion scarf which
might be the one he used to come flashing in front of Hazel
before he gave up this incipient paedophilia. Jill had a theory
that the scarf was not really to do with seduction tactics at all,
but useful in hiding his comical Adam's apple from the possible
giggling multitudes.

'You spoke of my quest, Col,' Iles murmured.

'True.'

'As, indeed, it is. I find it praiseworthy that once in a while
from your gravely limited vocabulary you will come up with
exactly the right word.'

'Thank you, sir.'

'However, we don't know, do we, what led to this killing, to

which you'll probably reply, "Led. Lead. What led to this killing
was the lead in what could be two .45 rounds to the chest, fired
from near enough for the blast to produce scorch marks on the
jogging garment, backgrounding the blood."'

Harpur said, 'Led. Lead, what led to this killing was the lead
in what could be two .45 rounds to the chest fired from near
enough for the blast to produce scorch marks on the jogging
garment, backgrounding the blood.'

'But I want to look wider, Col.'

'This is so typical of you, sir. Width is your home ground.
Why I mentioned individuality.'

'My quest, as you justly call it, is to do with finding those
responsible for the Shale deaths, Naomi and Laurent, on my
Sandicott ground. On *my* fucking Sandicott ground, Harpur.'

'Well, the chief's ground, also.'

'On *my* fucking Sandicott ground, Harpur. What's in the
brackets, Col?'

'In the brackets? Which?'

'What's my rank?'

'Well, Assistant Chief Constable.'

'What's in the brackets? What is it that defines this assistant
chief?'

'Ah!'

'You've triumphantly broken through to the obvious again,
have you?'

'You're Assistant Chief Constable, and then, in the brackets,
Operations: Assistant Chief Constable.' Harpur drew two brackets
in the air with his finger.

'Brill, Harpur! And Sandicott is, I think you'll agree, an
operation. The chief? We can leave him out of it. He's along
the corridor playing with his budget. Yes, indeed, Sandicott's
an operation and it's mine. But we cannot know as a certainty
that this latest death is connected with those. It *is* connected in
that all three resulted from bullet wounds. But it would be
unwise to press the similarity further. I wanted to talk to him.
The chance is gone.'

'Why I said "tricky", sir.'

'And if we do know, or come to know, this death is connected
somehow to the Shale murders we cannot look further, wider,

or, most importantly, higher, because the entity who might have been persuaded, and/or plea-bargained, to help us in that is here, dead on a dirt path, where, ironically, he sought fitness, among the rabbits and their stalkers, the chest of his jogging suit a mess because of those previously mentioned .45 bullets.'

'Didn't I read in the press somewhere about south of the Thames London firearms gangs favouring .45 Smith and Wessons?'

'We'll be told if these rounds come from an S&W.'

'This model is probably still available for purchase.'

'Yes, probably.'

'These various, competing, mutually cancelling items of information is why I selected that word, sir.'

'Which?'

'Tricky.'

As in the Binnacle, a small tent had been erected around the body. The police photographer arrived and went inside. Nearby, in a parked police van, Garland was talking to the two youths who had made the find, their tethered terriers yapping now and then.

An unmarked black BMW approached, Sergeant Pate driving. Rose Waverton and a WPC in the back. Harpur spoke through the front opening of the tent to the photographer, 'Leave it for a little while. His wife, widow, is here.' The photographer came out. Rose Waverton left the BMW and walked towards them. She looked as though she had dressed hurriedly – jeans, a cream crew-necked sweater under a black unbuttoned raincoat, flat brown shoes, no hat. Her nicely rounded face looked made for cheerfulness, but, of course, there was none of that present now. It had also been absent at first when she called at 126 Arthur Street following the gala. She said, 'Harpur, didn't you tell me the situation as regards Frank was simply routine and harmless?'

Oh God, yes he had done that. Denise helped him make it sound authentic. And it had worked, for the moment. The aim had been kindness, only that. They'd wanted to ease Rose Waverton's anxieties about her husband. They hadn't really understood then what Frank Waverton's role in all this had been. In fact, Harpur didn't understand *now* what that role

had been, supposing he'd had a role. Maybe someone somewhere knew, but if he or she existed that someone remained a
mystery someone, undiscoverable so far even by Iles on his
quest. The soothing explanation for the police interest in Frank
Waverton that Denise and Harpur had given her – a 'touchstone'
only, a 'paradigm' only–– had been short-termism: an attempt
to reassure her then and there that Frank was no special target
and would be available, if needed, for further love-making in
the back of the Mercedes. Could anyone have foreseen then
this swerve into havoc?

'We're very sorry, Mrs Waverton,' Iles said, 'but there have
been developments. If you ask Harpur he'll tell you. "Tricky."'

Harpur would have liked to tell her something more precise
than that but couldn't. These two visits – Mrs 'Vaughan' to
view her dead son, Mrs Waverton to view her dead husband
– he found depressingly, opaquely linked. What Denise has
been able to tell Garland and Harpur about the Binnacle violence
only confirmed statements from other witnesses. Denise could
help Harpur now and then, but not with this.

THIRTY

At the Monty, Ralph Ember took a phone call in his upstairs office. Shale, voice quivering with warmth, admiration and friendship, said, 'Congrats, Ralph. I'm not going to state no more for the usual very obvious reasons. But, remember, Ralphy, I'm in your debt, long-term or short. You'll find Manse Shale don't forget his obligations, but repays in similar, what you might say, coin.'

Ember put the phone down, confused, almost dazed. When he'd heard not long ago that Frank Waverton had been found shot in the chest on Torson Steep he had assumed Manse must have finally tired of waiting for Ralph to act and had done what he said he'd thought of doing at the Binnacle: complete the job himself. No. Not at all. Not Manse and certainly not himself. So, who?

During his university foundation year he'd heard of something called the *deus ex machina* in classical stage dramas, describing an unexpected intervention from outside that resolved all the problems created in the play, no matter how messy. Ralph had always admired those ancient writers. They produced their stuff ages ago, yet it could still apply to situations now, although they wouldn't have had any idea of what 'dawn jogging on Torson Steep' meant.

Ember would let the misunderstanding continue, of course. However, he did wonder what the moral implications might be. Would it be honourable at a future moment to call on Manse to slaughter someone for him, as per agreement, despite the fact that Ember had never fulfilled his part of it? Tricky.

But existentialism taught that random events could shatter all plans, and this had to be accepted. What happened at the Binnacle was random, as far as Ralph was concerned. He would accept it, gladly.

THIRTY-ONE

Iles didn't get to the funeral of Wyn Normanton Vaughan, so Harpur didn't, either. Garland went. But there was a Gospel Hall memorial service in Wales for young Vaughan later and they did attend that. Wyn's parents were clearly very touched that the two officers had made the journey.

This kind of ceremony was familiar to Harpur: he'd been brought up in a Gospel Hall Sunday School; that is, his parents sent him, though they never entered a church or chapel themselves. He recognized some of the texts inscribed on banners around the rigorously simple inside of the place: 'Without shedding of blood is no remission'; 'Those who seek me early shall find me.' The hymns he fancied, too. 'Just as I am without one plea'; 'Once I was dead in sin.'

The service was conducted by a middle-aged man in a collar and tie, dark suit and brown shoes. Gospel Halls did without vicars, priests or ministers.

Iles behaved dismally well, no heckling, no blasphemies, no kicking, no half nelsons or gouging, and this sickened and angered Harpur. It was as though some inner vitality and special, individual awfulness – yes, individual – had been removed from the ACC because of the failure to reach whoever ordered the Sandicott attack on his ground. On *his* fucking Sandicott ground. In one of the spells for silent meditation Harpur offered a kind of prayer, a plea, that the ACC might soon recover his natural, flavoursome spite, energy and glorious arrogance. Harpur hadn't worn the jockstrap or cricket box today because he'd felt a memorial service would probably not get Iles going in the way a funeral could. But Harpur had not expected this total, bewildering, passiveness.

Iles and Harpur spoke briefly at the close to Mr and Mrs Vaughan on the pavement outside. Gareth Leo Vaughan said, 'I heard you had further violent trouble in your manor.'

'Yes,' Iles said. 'Unsolved. Unsolvable?'

'That guy, Waverton, killed by .45 rounds. Those are big bullets, big wounds,' Vaughan said.

'Do you know anything about that sort of thing?' Iles replied.

'You wouldn't expect us to be upset, would you?' Mrs Vaughan said. 'It's good to know he'll supply no more.'

'No more drugs?' Iles replied. 'You're entirely anti them, are you? Well, the debate will continue.'

'Knives,' she said. 'I meant no more knives.'

'It's a mixed-up situation,' Harpur said.

'I'd call it closure,' Vaughan said.

'But, Col has a different word for it.'

'Yes?' Catrin Vaughan said.

'Tricky,' Iles said.